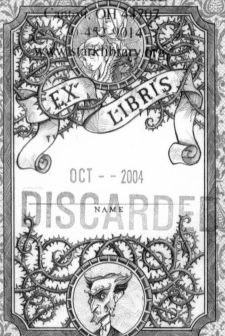

THE CARNIVOROUS CARNIVAL

⚹ A Series of Unfortunate Events ⚹

THE BAD BEGINNING
⚹
THE REPTILE ROOM
⚹
THE WIDE WINDOW
⚹
THE MISERABLE MILL
⚹
THE AUSTERE ACADEMY
⚹
THE ERSATZ ELEVATOR
⚹
THE VILE VILLAGE
⚹
THE HOSTILE HOSPITAL
⚹
THE CARNIVOROUS CARNIVAL

* A Series of Unfortunate Events *

BOOK the Ninth

THE CARNIVOROUS CARNIVAL

by LEMONY SNICKET

Illustrations by Brett Helquist

HarperCollinsPublishers

❄

Library of Congress Cataloging-in-Publication Data
Snicket, Lemony.
    The carnivorous carnival / by Lemony Snicket ; illustrations by Brett
Helquist.
        p.   cm. — (A series of unfortunate events ; bk. 9)
    Summary: On the run as suspected murderers, the unlucky Baudelaire
orphans find themselves trapped in the Caligari Carnival, where they must
masquerade as freaks in order to hide from the evil Count Olaf.
    ISBN 0-06-441012-9 — ISBN 0-06-029640-2 (lib. bdg.)
    [1. Orphans—Fiction. 2. Brothers and sisters—Fiction. 3. Carnivals—
Fiction. 4. Humorous stories.] I. Helquist, Brett, ill. II. Title.
PZ7.S6795 Car   2003   2002008337
[Fic]—dc21   CIP
                                                                      AC

7   9   11   13   15   17   16   14   12   10   8
❖
First Edition, 2002
Visit us on the World Wide Web! www.harperchildrens.com

❄

For Beatrice—
Our love broke my heart,
and stopped yours.

THE CARNIVOROUS CARNIVAL

One

When my workday is over, and I have closed my notebook, hidden my pen, and sawed holes in my rented canoe so that it cannot be found, I often like to spend the evening in conversation with my few surviving friends. Sometimes we discuss literature. Sometimes we discuss the people who are trying to destroy us, and if there is any hope of escaping from them. And sometimes we discuss frightening and troublesome animals that might be nearby, and this topic always leads to much disagreement over which part of a frightening and troublesome beast is the most frightening and troublesome. Some say the teeth of the beast, because teeth are used for eating children, and often their parents, and gnawing their bones. Some say the claws of the beast, because claws are used for ripping things to shreds. And some say the hair of the beast, because hair can make allergic people sneeze.

But I always insist that the most frightening part of any beast is its belly, for the simple reason that if you are seeing the belly of the beast it means you have already seen the teeth of the beast and the claws of the beast and even the hair of the beast, and now you are trapped and there is probably no hope for you. For this reason, the phrase "in the belly of the beast" has become an expression which means "inside some terrible place with little chance of escaping safely," and it is not an expression one should look forward to using.

I'm sorry to tell you that this book will use the expression "the belly of the beast" three times before it is over, not counting all of the times I have already used "the belly of the beast" in order to warn you of all the times "the belly of the beast" will appear. Three times over the course of this story, characters will be inside some terrible place with little chance of escaping safely, and for that reason I would put this book down and escape safely yourself, because this woeful story is so very dark and wretched and damp that the experience of reading it will make you feel as if you are in the belly of the beast, and that time doesn't count either.

The Baudelaire orphans were in the belly of the beast—that is, in the dark and cramped trunk of a long, black automobile. Unless you are a small, portable object, you probably prefer to sit in a seat when you are traveling by automobile, so you can lean back against the upholstery, look out the window at the scenery going by, and feel safe and secure with a seat belt fastened low and tight across your lap. But the Baudelaires could not lean back, and their bodies were aching from squishing up against one another for several hours. They had no window to look out of, only a few bullet holes in the trunk made from some violent encounter I have not found the courage to research. And they felt anything but safe and secure as they thought about the other passengers in the car, and tried to imagine where they were going.

The driver of the automobile was a man named Count Olaf, a wicked person with one eyebrow instead of two and a greedy desire for money instead of respect for other people. The Baudelaires had first met Count Olaf after receiving the news that their parents had been killed in a terrible fire, and had soon discovered he was only interested in the enormous fortune their mother and father had left behind. With unceasing determination—a phrase which here means "no matter where the three children went"—Count Olaf had pursued them, trying one dastardly technique after another to get his hands on their fortune. So far he had been unsuccessful, although he'd had plenty of help from his girlfriend, Esmé Squalor—an equally wicked, if more fashionable, person who was now sitting beside him in the front seat of the automobile—and an assortment of assistants, including a bald man with an enormous nose, two women who liked to wear white powder all over their faces, and a nasty man who had hooks instead of hands. All of these people were sitting in the back of the automobile, where the children could sometimes hear them speaking over the roar of the engine and the sounds of the road.

One would think, with such a wretched crew as traveling companions, that the Baudelaire siblings would have found some other way to travel rather than sneaking into the trunk, but the three children had been fleeing from circumstances even more frightening and dangerous than Olaf and his assistants and there had been no time to be choosy. But as their journey wore on, Violet, Klaus, and Sunny grew more and more worried about their situation. The sunlight coming in through the bullet holes faded to evening, and the road beneath them turned bumpy and rough, and the Baudelaire orphans tried to imagine where it was they were going and what would happen when they got there.

"Are we there yet?" The voice of the hook-handed man broke a long silence.

"I told you not to ask me that anymore," replied Olaf with a snarl. "We'll get there when we get there, and that is that."

"Could we possibly make a short stop?" asked one of the white-faced women. "I noticed a sign for a rest station in a few miles."

"We don't have time to stop anywhere," Olaf said sharply. "If you needed to use the bathroom, you should have gone before we left."

"But the hospital was on fire," the woman whined.

"Yes, let's stop," said the bald man. "We haven't had anything to eat since lunch, and my stomach is grumbling."

"We can't stop," Esmé said. "There are no restaurants out here in the hinterlands that are in."

Violet, who was the eldest of the Baudelaires, stretched to place her hand on Klaus's stiff shoulder, and held her baby sister, Sunny, even tighter, as if to communicate with her siblings without speaking. Esmé Squalor was constantly talking about whether or not things were in—a word she liked to use for "stylish"—but the children were more interested in overhearing where the car was taking them. The hinterlands were a vast and empty place very far from the very outskirts of the city, without even a small village for hundreds of miles. Long ago the Baudelaire parents had promised they would bring their children there someday to see the famous hinterlands sunsets. Klaus, who was a voracious reader, had read descriptions of the sunsets that had made the whole family eager to go, and Violet, who had a real talent for inventing things, had even begun building a solar oven so the family could enjoy grilled cheese sandwiches as they watched the dark blue light spread eerily over the hinterlands cacti while the sun slowly sank behind the distant and frosty Mortmain Mountains. Never did the three siblings imagine that they would visit the hinterlands by themselves, stuffed in the trunk of a car of a villain.

"Boss, are you sure it's safe to be way out here?" asked the hook-handed man. "If the police come looking for us, there'll be no place to hide."

"We could always disguise ourselves again," the bald man said. "Everything we need is in the trunk of the car.

"We don't need to hide," Olaf replied, "and we don't need to disguise ourselves, either. Thanks to that silly reporter at *The Daily Punctilio*, the whole world thinks I'm dead, remember?"

"You're dead," Esmé said with a nasty chuckle, "and the three Baudelaire brats are murderers. We don't need to hide—we need to celebrate!"

"We can't celebrate yet," Olaf said. "There

are two last things we need to do. First, we need
to destroy the last piece of evidence that could
send us to jail."

"The Snicket file," Esmé said, and the
Baudelaires shuddered in the trunk. The three
children had found one page of the Snicket file,
which was now safe in Klaus's pocket. It was difficult to tell from only one page, but the Snicket
file seemed to contain information about a survivor of a fire, and the Baudelaires were eager
to find the remaining pages before Olaf did.

"Yes, of course," the hook-handed man said.
"We have to find the Snicket file. But what's the
second thing?"

"We have to find the Baudelaires, you idiot,"
Olaf snarled. "If we don't find them, then we
can't steal their fortune, and all of my schemes
will be a waste."

"I haven't found your schemes to be a
waste," said one of the white-faced women.
"I've enjoyed them very much, even if we
haven't gotten the fortune."

"Do you think all three of those bratty orphans got out of the hospital alive?" the bald man asked.

"Those children seem to have all the luck in the world," Count Olaf said, "so they're all probably alive and well, but it would sure make things easier if one or two of them burned to a crisp. We only need one of them alive to get the fortune."

"I hope it's Sunny," the hook-handed man said. "It was fun putting her in a cage, and I look forward to doing it again."

"I myself hope it's Violet," Olaf said. "She's the prettiest."

"I don't care who it is," Esmé said. "I just want to know where they are."

"Well, Madame Lulu will know," Olaf said. "With her crystal ball, she'll be able to tell us where the orphans are, where the file is, and anything else we want to know."

"I never believed in things like crystal balls," remarked a white-faced woman, "but when this

Madame Lulu started telling you how to find the Baudelaires every time they escaped, I learned that fortune-telling is real."

"Stick with me," Olaf said, "and you'll learn lots of new things. Oh, here's the turn for Rarely Ridden Road. We're almost there."

The car lurched to the left, and the Baudelaires lurched with it, rolling to the left-hand side of the trunk, along with the many items Olaf kept in his car to help with his dastardly plots. Violet tried not to cough as one of his fake beards tickled her throat. Klaus held his hand up to his face so that a sliding toolbox wouldn't break his glasses. And Sunny shut her mouth tightly so she wouldn't get one of Olaf's dirty undershirts tangled in her sharp teeth. Rarely Ridden Road was even bumpier than the highway they had been traveling on, and the car made so much noise that the children could not hear any more of the conversation until Olaf pulled the automobile to a creaky stop.

"Are we there yet?" the hook-handed man asked.

"Of course we're here, you fool," Olaf said. "Look, there's the sign—Caligari Carnival."

"Where is Madame Lulu?" asked the bald man.

"Where do you think?" Esmé asked, and everyone laughed. The doors of the automobile opened with a scraping sound, and the car lurched again as everyone piled out.

"Should I get the wine out of the trunk, boss?" the bald man asked.

The Baudelaires froze.

"No," Count Olaf replied. "Madame Lulu will have plenty of refreshments for us."

The three children lay very still and listened as Olaf and his troupe trudged away from the car. Their footsteps grew fainter and fainter until the siblings could hear nothing but the evening breeze as it whistled through the bullet holes, and at last it seemed safe for the Baudelaire orphans to speak to one another.

"What are we going to do?" Violet whispered, pushing the beard away from her.

"Merrill," Sunny said. Like many people her age, the youngest Baudelaire sometimes used language that was difficult for some people to understand, but her siblings knew at once that she meant something like, "We'd better get out of this trunk."

"As soon as possible," Klaus agreed. "We don't know how soon Olaf and his troupe will return. Violet, do you think you can invent something to get us out of here?"

"It shouldn't be too hard," Violet said, "with all this stuff in the trunk." She reached out her hand and felt around until she found the mechanism that was keeping the trunk closed. "I've studied this kind of latch before," she said. "All I need to move it is a loop of strong twine. Feel around and see if we can find something."

"There's something wrapped around my left arm," Klaus said, squirming around. "It feels like it might be part of the turban Olaf wore when he disguised himself as Coach Genghis."

"That's too thick," Violet said. "It needs to slip between two parts of the lock."

"Semja!" Sunny said.

"That's my shoelace, Sunny," Klaus said.

"We'll save that as a last resort," Violet said. "We can't have you tripping all over the place if we're going to escape. Wait, I think I found something underneath the spare tire."

"What is it?"

"I don't know," Violet said. "It feels like a skinny cord with something round and flat at the end."

"I bet it's a monocle," Klaus said. "You know, that funny eyepiece Olaf wore when he was pretending to be Gunther, the auctioneer."

"I think you're right," Violet said. "Well, this monocle helped Olaf with his scheme, and now it's going to help us with ours. Sunny, try to move over a bit so I can see if this will work."

Sunny squirmed over as far as she could, and Violet reached around her siblings and slipped the cord of Olaf's monocle around the lock of the trunk. The three children listened as Violet wiggled her invention around the latch, and after only a few seconds they heard a quiet *click!* and the door of the trunk swung open with a long, slow *creeeak*. As the cool air rushed in, the Baudelaires stayed absolutely still in case the noise of the trunk caught Olaf's attention, but apparently he and his assistants were too far away to hear, because after a few seconds the children could hear nothing but the chirping of the evening crickets and the faint barking of a dog.

The Baudelaires looked at one another, squinting in the dim light, and without another word Violet and Klaus climbed out of the trunk and then lifted their sister out into the night. The famous hinterlands sunset was just ending, and everything the children saw was bathed in dark blue, as if Count Olaf had driven them into the depths of the ocean. There was a large wooden sign with the words CALIGARI CARNIVAL printed in old-fashioned script, along with a faded painting of a lion chasing a frightened little boy. Behind the sign was a small booth advertising tickets for sale, and a phone booth that gleamed in the blue light. Behind these two booths was an enormous roller coaster, a phrase which here means "a series of small carts where people can sit and race up and down steep and frightening hills of tracks, for no discernible reason," but it was clear, even in the fading light, that the roller coaster had not been used for quite some time, because the tracks and carts were overgrown with ivy and other winding plants, which made the carnival attraction look as if it were about to sink into the earth. Past the roller coaster was a row of enormous tents, shivering in the evening breeze like jellyfish, and alongside each tent was a caravan, which is a wheeled carriage used as a home by people who travel frequently. The caravans and tents all had different designs painted on the sides, but the Baudelaires knew at once which caravan was Madame Lulu's because it was decorated with an enormous eye. The eye matched the one tattooed on Count Olaf's left ankle, the one the Baudelaires had seen many times in their lives, and it made them shiver to think they could not escape it even in the hinterlands.

"Now that we're out of the trunk," Klaus said, "let's get out of the area. Olaf and his troupe could get back any minute."

"But where are we going to go?" Violet asked. "We're in the hinterlands. Olaf's comrade said there was no place to hide."

"Well, we'll have to find one," Klaus said. "It can't be safe to hang around any place where Count Olaf is welcome."

"Eye!" Sunny agreed, pointing to Madame Lulu's caravan.

"But we can't go wandering around the countryside again," Violet said. "The last time we did that, we ended up in even more trouble."

"Maybe we could call the police from that

phone booth," Klaus said.

"Dragnet!" Sunny said, which meant "But the police think we're murderers!"

"I suppose we could try to reach Mr. Poe," Violet said. "He didn't answer the telegram we sent him asking for help, but maybe we'll have better luck on the phone."

The three siblings looked at one another without much hope. Mr. Poe was the Vice President of Orphan Affairs at Mulctuary Money Management, a large bank in the city, and part of his job was overseeing the Baudelaires' affairs after the fire. Mr. Poe was not a wicked person, but he had mistakenly placed them in the company of so much wickedness that he had been almost as wicked as an actual wicked person, and the children were not particularly eager to contact him again, even if it was all they could think of.

"It's probably a slim chance that he'll be of any help," Violet admitted, "but what have we got to lose?"

"Let's not think about that," Klaus replied, and walked over to the phone booth. "Maybe Mr. Poe will at least allow us to explain ourselves."

"Veriz," Sunny said, which meant something like, "We'll need money to make a phone call."

"I don't have any," Klaus said, reaching into his pockets. "Do you have any money, Violet?"

Violet shook her head. "Let's call the operator and see if there's some way we can place a call without paying for it."

Klaus nodded, and opened the door of the booth so he and his sisters could crowd inside. Violet lifted the receiver and dialed O for operator, while Klaus lifted up Sunny so all three siblings could hear the conversation.

"Operator," said the operator.

"Good evening," Violet said. "My siblings and I would like to place a call."

"Please deposit the proper amount of money," the operator said.

"We don't have the proper amount of money," Violet said. "We don't have any money at all. But this is an emergency."

There was a faint wheezing noise from the phone, and the Baudelaires realized that the operator was sighing. "What is the exact nature of your emergency?"

Violet looked down at her siblings and saw the last of the sunset's blue light reflecting off Klaus's glasses and Sunny's teeth. As the dark closed around them, the nature of their emergency seemed so enormous that it would take the rest of the night to explain it to the telephone operator, and the eldest Baudelaire tried to figure out how she could summarize, a word which here means "tell their story in a way that would convince the operator to let them talk to Mr. Poe."

"Well," she began, "my name is Violet Baudelaire, and I'm here with my brother, Klaus, and my sister, Sunny. Our names might sound a bit familiar to you, because *The Daily Punctilio* has recently published an article saying that we're Veronica, Klyde, and Susie Baudelaire, and that we're murderers who killed Count Omar. But Count Omar is really Count Olaf, and he's not really dead. He faked his death by killing another person with the same tattoo, and framed us for the murder. Recently he destroyed a hospital while trying to capture us, but we managed to hide in the trunk of his car as he drove off with his comrades. Now we've gotten out of the trunk, and we're trying to reach Mr. Poe so he can help us get ahold of the Snicket file, which we think might explain what the initials V.F.D. stand for, and if one of our parents survived the fire after all. I know it's a very complicated story, and it may seem unbelievable to you, but we're all by ourselves in the hinterlands and we don't know what else to do."

The story was so terrible that Violet had cried a little while telling it, and she brushed a tear from her eye as she waited for a reply from the operator. But no voice came out of the phone.

The three Baudelaires listened carefully, but all they could hear was the empty and distant sound of a telephone line.

"Hello?" Violet said finally.

The telephone said nothing.

"Hello?" Violet said again. "Hello? Hello?"

The telephone did not answer.

"*Hello?*" Violet said, as loud as she dared.

"I think we'd better hang up," Klaus said gently.

"But why isn't anyone answering?" Violet cried.

"I don't know," Klaus said, "but I don't think the operator will help us."

Violet hung up the phone and opened the door of the booth. Now that the sun was down the air was getting colder, and she shivered in the evening breeze. "Who will help us?" she asked. "Who will take care of us?"

"We'll have to take care of ourselves," Klaus said.

"Ephrai," Sunny said, which meant "But

we're in real trouble now."

"We sure are," Violet agreed. "We're in the middle of nowhere, with no place to hide, and the whole world thinks we're criminals. How do criminals take care of themselves out in the hinterlands?"

The Baudelaires heard a burst of laughter, as if in reply. The laughter was quite faint, but in the still of the evening it made the children jump. Sunny pointed, and the children could see a light in one of the windows in Madame Lulu's caravan. Several shadows moved across the window, and the children could tell that Count Olaf and his troupe were inside, chatting and laughing while the Baudelaire orphans shivered outside in the gloom.

"Let's go see," Klaus said. "Let's go find out how criminals take care of themselves."

Eavesdropping—a word which here means "listening in on interesting conversations you are not invited to join"—is a valuable thing to do, and it is often an enjoyable thing to do, but it is not a polite thing to do, and like most impolite things, you are bound to get into trouble if you get caught doing it. The Baudelaire orphans, of course, had plenty of experience not getting caught, so the three children knew how to walk as quietly as possible across the grounds of Caligari Carnival, and how to crouch as invisibly as possible outside the window of Madame Lulu's caravan. If you had been there that eerie blue evening—and nothing in my research indicates that you were—you wouldn't have heard even the slightest rustle from the Baudelaires as they eavesdropped on their enemies.

Count Olaf and his troupe, however, were making plenty of noise. "Madame Lulu!" Count Olaf was roaring as the children pressed up against the side of the caravan so that they would be hidden in the shadows. "Madame Lulu, pour us some wine! Arson and escaping from the authorities always makes me very thirsty!"

"I'd prefer buttermilk, served in a paper carton," Esmé said. "That's the new in beverage."

"Five glasses of wine and a carton of buttermilk coming up, please," answered a woman in an accent the children recognized. Not so long ago, when Esmé Squalor had been the

Baudelaires' caretaker, Olaf had disguised himself as a person who did not speak English well, and as part of his disguise, he had spoken in an accent very similar to the one they were hearing now. The Baudelaires tried to peer through the window and catch a glimpse of the fortuneteller, but Madame Lulu had shut her curtains tightly. "I'm thrilled, please, to see you, my Olaf. Welcome to the caravan of mine. How is life for you?"

"We've been swamped at work," the hookhanded man said, using a phrase which here means "chasing after innocent children for quite some time." "Those three orphans have been very difficult to capture."

"Do not worry of the children, please," Madame Lulu replied. "My crystal ball tells me that my Olaf will prevail."

"If that means 'murder innocent children,'" one of the white-faced women said, "then that's the best news we've heard all day."

"'Prevail' means 'win,'" Olaf said, "but in my

case that's the same thing as killing those Baudelaires. Exactly when does the crystal ball say I will prevail, Lulu?"

"Very soon, please," Madame Lulu replied. "What gifts have you brought me from your traveling, my Olaf?"

"Well, let's see," Olaf replied. "There's a lovely pearl necklace I stole from one of the nurses at Heimlich Hospital."

"You promised me *I* could have that," Esmé said. "Give her one of those crow hats you snatched from the Village of Fowl Devotees."

"I tell you, Lulu," Olaf said, "your fortune-telling abilities are amazing. I never would have guessed that the Baudelaires were hiding out in that stupid town, but your crystal ball knew right away."

"Magic is magic, please," Lulu replied. "More wine, my Olaf?"

"Thank you," Olaf said. "Now, Lulu, we need your fortune-telling abilities once more."

"The Baudelaire brats slipped away from us

again," the bald man said, "and the boss was hoping you'd be able to tell us where they went."

"Also," the hook-handed man said, "we need to know where the Snicket file is."

"And we need to know if one of the Baudelaire parents survived the fire," Esmé said. "The orphans seem to think so, but your crystal ball could tell us for sure."

"And I'd like some more wine," one of the white-faced women said.

"So many demands you make," Madame Lulu said in her strange accent. "Madame Lulu remembers, please, when you would visit only for the pleasure of my company, my Olaf."

"There isn't time for that tonight," Olaf replied quickly. "Can't you consult your crystal ball right now?"

"You know rules of crystal ball, my Olaf," Lulu replied. "At night the crystal ball must be sleeping in the fortune-telling tent, and at sunrise you may ask one question."

"Then I'll ask my first question tomorrow morning," Olaf said, "and we'll stay until all my questions are answered."

"Oh, my Olaf," Madame Lulu said. "Please, times are very hard for Caligari Carnival. Is not good business idea to have carnival in hinterlands, so there are not many people to see Madame Lulu or crystal ball. Caligari Carnival gift caravan has lousy souvenirs. And Madame Lulu has not enough freaks, please, in the House of Freaks. You visit, my Olaf, with troupe, and stay many days, drink my wine and eat all of my snackings."

"This roast chicken is very delicious," the hook-handed man said.

"Madame Lulu has no money, please," Lulu continued. "Is hard, my Olaf, to do fortune-telling for you when Madame Lulu is so poor. The caravan of mine has leaky roof, and Madame Lulu needs money, please, to do repairs."

"I've told you before," Olaf said, "once we

get the Baudelaire fortune, the carnival will have plenty of money."

"You said that about Quagmire fortune, my Olaf," Madame Lulu said, "and about Snicket fortune. But never a penny does Madame Lulu see. We must think, please, of something to make Caligari Carnival more popular. Madame Lulu was hoping that troupe of my Olaf could put on a big show like *The Marvelous Marriage*. Many people would come to see."

"The boss can't get up on stage," the bald man said. "Planning schemes is a full-time job."

"Besides," Esmé said, "I've retired from show business. All I want to be now is Count Olaf's girlfriend."

There was a silence, and the only thing the Baudelaires could hear from Lulu's caravan was the crunch of someone chewing on chicken bones. Then there was a long sigh, and Lulu spoke very quietly. "You did not tell me, my Olaf, that Esmé was the girlfriend of you. Perhaps Madame Lulu will not let you and troupe stay at the carnival of mine."

"Now, now, Lulu," Count Olaf said, and the children shivered as they eavesdropped. Olaf was talking in a tone of voice the Baudelaires had heard many times, when he was trying to fool someone into thinking he was a kind and decent person. Even with the curtains closed, the Baudelaires could tell that he was giving Madame Lulu a toothy grin, and that his eyes were shining brightly beneath his one eyebrow, as if he were about to tell a joke. "Did I ever tell you how I began my career as an actor?"

"It's a fascinating story," the hook-handed man said.

"It certainly is," Olaf agreed. "Give me some more wine, and I'll tell you. Now then, as a child, I was always the most handsome fellow at school, and one day a young director . . ."

The Baudelaires had heard enough. The three children had spent enough time with the villain to know that once he began talking about himself, he continued until the cows came home, a phrase which here means "until there was no more wine," and they tiptoed away from Madame Lulu's caravan and back toward Count Olaf's car so they could talk without being overheard. In the dark of night, the long, black automobile looked like an enormous hole, and the children felt as if they were about to fall into it as they tried to decide what to do.

"I guess we should leave," Klaus said uncertainly. "It's definitely not safe around here, but I don't know where we can go in the hinterlands. There's nothing for miles and miles but wilderness, and we could die of thirst, or be attacked by wild animals."

Violet looked around quickly, as if something were about to attack them that very moment, but the only wild animal in view was the painted lion on the carnival sign. "Even if we found someone else out there," she said, "they'd probably think we were murderers and call the police. Also, Madame Lulu promised to answer all of Olaf's questions tomorrow morning."

"You don't think Madame Lulu's crystal ball really works, do you?" Klaus asked. "I've never read any evidence that fortune-telling is real."

"But Madame Lulu keeps telling Count Olaf where we are," Violet pointed out. "She must be getting her information from some-place. If she can really find out the location of the Snicket file, or learn if one of our parents is alive . . ."

Her voice trailed off, but she did not need to finish her sentence. All three Baudelaires knew that finding out if someone survived the fire was worth the risk of staying nearby.

"Sandover," Sunny said, which meant "So we're staying."

"We should at least stay the night," Klaus agreed. "But where can we hide? If we don't stay out of sight, someone is likely to recog-nize us."

"Karneez?" Sunny asked.

"The people in those caravans work for Ma-dame Lulu," Klaus said. "Who knows if they'd help us or not?"

"I have an idea," Violet said, and walked over to the back of Count Olaf's car. With a *creeeak*, she opened the trunk again and leaned down inside.

"Nuts!" Sunny said, which meant "I don't think that's such a good idea, Violet."

"Sunny's right," Klaus said. "Olaf and his henchmen might come back any minute to unpack the trunk. We can't hide in there."

"We're not going to hide in there," Violet said. "We're not going to hide at all. After all, Olaf and his troupe never hide, and they manage not to be recognized. We're going to disguise ourselves."

"Gabrowha?" Sunny asked.

"Why wouldn't it work?" Violet replied. "Olaf wears these disguises and he manages to fool everyone. If we fool Madame Lulu into thinking we're somebody else, we can stay around and find the answers to our questions."

"It seems risky," Klaus said, "but I suppose

it's just as risky as trying to hide someplace. Who should we pretend to be?"

"Let's look through the disguises," Violet said, "and see if we get any ideas."

"We'll have to feel through them," Klaus said. "It's too dark to look through anything."

The Baudelaires stood in front of the open trunk and reached inside to begin their search. As I'm sure you know, whenever you are examining someone else's belongings, you are bound to learn many interesting things about the person of which you were not previously aware. You might examine some letters your sister received recently, for instance, and learn that she was planning on running away with an archduke. You might examine the suitcases of another passenger on a train you are taking, and learn that he had been secretly photographing you for the past six months. I recently looked in the refrigerator of one of my enemies and learned she was a vegetarian, or at least pretending to be one, or had a vegetarian visiting her for a few days. And as the Baudelaire orphans examined some of the objects in Olaf's trunk, they learned a great deal of unpleasant things. Violet found part of a brass lamp she remembered from living with Uncle Monty, and learned that Olaf had stolen from her poor guardian, in addition to murdering him. Klaus found a large shopping bag from the In Boutique, and learned that Esmé Squalor was just as obsessed with fashionable clothing as she ever was. And Sunny found a pair of pantyhose covered in sawdust, and learned that Olaf had not washed his receptionist disguise since he had used it last. But the most dismaying thing the children learned from searching the trunk of Olaf's car was just how many disguises he had at his disposal. They found the hat Olaf used to disguise himself as a ship captain, and the razor he had probably used to shave his head in order to resemble a lab assistant. They found the expensive running shoes he had worn to disguise himself as a gym teacher, and the plastic ones he had used when he was pretending to be a detective. But the siblings also found plenty of costumes they had never seen before, and it seemed as though Olaf could keep on disguising himself forever, following the Baudelaires to location after location, always appearing with a new identity and never getting caught.

"We could disguise ourselves as almost anybody," Violet said. "Look, here's a wig that makes me look like a clown, and here's one that makes me look like a judge."

"I know," Klaus said, holding up a large box with several drawers. "This appears to be a makeup kit, complete with fake mustaches, fake eyebrows, and even a pair of glass eyes."

"Twicho!" Sunny said, holding up a long white veil.

"No, thank you," Violet said. "I already had to wear that veil once, when Olaf nearly married me. I'd rather not wear it again. Besides, what would a bride be doing wandering around the hinterlands?"

"Look at this long robe," Klaus said. "It looks

like something a rabbi would wear, but I don't know if Madame Lulu would believe that a rabbi would visit her in the middle of the night."

"Ginawn!" Sunny said, using her teeth to wrap a pair of sweatpants around her. The youngest Baudelaire meant something like, "All these clothes are too big for me," and she was right.

"That's even bigger than that pinstripe suit Esmé bought you," Klaus said, helping his sister get disentangled. "No one would believe that a pair of sweatpants was walking around a carnival by itself."

"All these clothes are too big," Violet said. "Look at this beige coat. If I tried to disguise myself in it, I'd only look freakish."

"Freakish!" Klaus said. "That's it!"

"Whazit?" Sunny asked.

"Madame Lulu said that she didn't have enough freaks in the House of Freaks. If we find disguises that make us look freakish, and tell Lulu that we're looking for work, she might hire us as part of the carnival."

"But what exactly do freaks do?" Violet asked.

"I read a book once about a man named John Merrick," Klaus said. "He had horrible birth defects that made him look terribly deformed. A carnival put him on display as part of a House of Freaks, and people paid money to go into a tent and look at him."

"Why would people want to look at someone with birth defects?" Violet asked. "It sounds cruel."

"It was cruel," Klaus said. "The crowd often threw things at Mr. Merrick, and called him names. I'm afraid the House of Freaks isn't a very pleasant form of entertainment."

"You'd think someone would put a stop to it," Violet said, "but you'd think somebody would put a stop to Count Olaf, too, and nobody does."

"Radev," Sunny said with a nervous look

around them. By "Radev," she meant "Some-body's going to put a stop to *us* if we don't dis-guise ourselves soon," and her siblings nodded solemnly in agreement.

"Here's some kind of fancy shirt," Klaus said. "It's covered in ruffles and bows. And here's an enormous pair of pants with fur on the cuffs."

"Could both of us wear them at once?" Violet asked.

"Both of us?" Klaus said. "I suppose so, if we kept on our clothes underneath, so Olaf's would fit. We could each stand on one leg, and tuck our other legs inside. We'd have to lean against one another as we walked, but I think it might work."

"And we could do the same thing with the shirt," Violet said. "We could each put one arm through a sleeve and keep the other tucked inside."

"But we couldn't hide one of our heads," Klaus pointed out, "and with both of our heads poking out of the top we'd look like some sort of—"

"—two-headed person," Violet finished, "and a two-headed person is exactly what a House of Freaks would put on display."

"That's good thinking," Klaus said. "People won't be on the lookout for a two-headed person. But we'll need to disguise our faces, too."

"The makeup kit will take care of that," Violet said. "Mother taught me how to draw fake scars on myself when she appeared in that play about the murderer."

"And here's a can of talcum powder," Klaus said. "We can use this to whiten our hair."

"Do you think Count Olaf will notice that these things are missing from his trunk?" Violet asked.

"I doubt it," Klaus said. "The trunk isn't very well organized, and I don't think he's used some of these disguises for a long time. I think we can take enough to become a two-headed person without Olaf missing anything."

"Beriu?" Sunny said, which meant "What about me?"

"These disguises are made for fully grown people," Violet said, "but I'm sure we can find you something. Maybe you could fit inside one of these shoes, and be a person with just a head and one foot. That's plenty freakish."

"Chelish," Sunny said, which meant something along the lines of, "I'm too big to fit inside a shoe."

"That's true," Klaus said. "It's been a while since you were shoe-sized." He reached inside the trunk and pulled out something short and hairy, as if he had caught a raccoon. "But this might work," he said. "I think this is the fake beard Olaf wore when he was pretending to be Stephano. It's a long beard, so it might work as a short disguise."

"Let's find out," Violet said, "and let's find out quickly."

The Baudelaires found out quickly. In just a few minutes, the children found out just how easy it was to transform themselves into entirely different people. Violet, Klaus, and Sunny had some experience in disguising themselves, of course—Klaus and Sunny had used medical coats at Heimlich Hospital in a plan to rescue Violet, and even Sunny could remember when all three siblings had occasionally worn costumes for their own amusement, back when they had lived in the Baudelaire mansion with their parents. But this time, the Baudelaire orphans felt more like Count Olaf and his troupe, as they worked quietly and hurriedly in the night to erase all traces of their true identities. Violet felt through the makeup kit until she found several pencils that were normally used to make one's eyebrows more dramatic, and even though it was simple and painless to draw scars on Klaus's face, it felt as if she were breaking the promise she made to her parents, a very long time ago, that she would always look after her siblings and keep them away from harm. Klaus helped Sunny wrap herself in Olaf's fake beard, but when he saw her eyes and the tips of her teeth peeking out of the mass of scratchy hair, it felt as if he had fed his baby sister to some tiny but hungry animal. And as Sunny helped her siblings button themselves into the fancy shirt and sprinkle talcum on their hair to turn it gray, it felt as if they were melting into Olaf's clothes. The three Baudelaires looked at one another carefully but it was as if there were no Baudelaires there at all, just two strangers, one with two heads and the other with a head that was covered in fur, all alone in the hinterlands.

"I think we look utterly unrecognizable," Klaus said, turning with difficulty to face his older sister. "Maybe it's because I took off my glasses, but to me we don't look a thing like ourselves."

"Will you be able to see without your glasses?" Violet asked.

"If I squint," Klaus said, squinting. "I can't read like this, but I won't be bumping into things. If I keep them on, Count Olaf will probably recognize me."

"Then you'd better keep them off," Violet said, "and I'll stop wearing a ribbon in my hair."

"We'd better disguise our voices, too," Klaus said. "I'll try to speak as high as I can, and why don't you try to speak in a low voice, Violet?"

"Good idea," Violet said, in as low a voice as she could. "And Sunny, you should probably just growl."

"Grr," Sunny tried.

"You sound like a wolf," Violet said, still practicing her disguised tone. "Let's tell Madame Lulu that you're half wolf and half person."

"That would be a miserable experience," Klaus said, in the highest voice he could manage. "But I suppose being born with two heads wouldn't be any easier."

"We'll explain to Lulu that we've had miserable experiences, but now we're hoping things will get better working at the carnival," Violet said, and then sighed. "That's one thing we don't have to pretend. We *have* had miserable experiences, and we *are* hoping that things will get better here. We're almost as freakish as we're pretending to be."

"Don't say that," Klaus said, and then remembered his new voice. "Don't say that," he said again, at a much higher pitch. "We're not freaks. We're still the Baudelaires, even if we're wearing Olaf's disguises."

"I know," Violet said, in her new voice, "but it's a little confusing pretending to be a completely different person."

"Grr," Sunny growled in agreement, and the three children put the rest of Count Olaf's things back in the trunk, and walked in silence to Madame Lulu's caravan. It was awkward for Violet and Klaus to walk in the same pair of pants, and Sunny had to keep stopping to brush the beard out of her eyes. It *was* confusing pretending to be completely different people, particularly because it had been so long since the Baudelaires were able to be the people they really were. Violet, Klaus, and Sunny did not think of themselves as the sort of children who hid in the trunks of automobiles, or who wore disguises, or who tried to get jobs at the House of Freaks. But the siblings could scarcely re-member when they had been able to relax and do the things they liked to do best. It seemed ages since Violet had been able to sit around and think of inventions, instead of frantically build-ing something to get them out of trouble. Klaus could barely remember the last book he had read for his own enjoyment, instead of as research to defeat one of Olaf's schemes. And Sunny had used her teeth many, many times to escape from difficult situations, but it had been quite a while since she had bitten something recreationally. As the youngsters approached the caravan, it seemed as if each awkward step took them further and further from their real lives as Baudelaires, and into their disguised lives as car-nival freaks, and it was indeed very confusing. When Sunny knocked on the door, Madame

Lulu called out, "Who's there?" and for the first time in their lives, it was a confusing question.

"We're freaks," Violet answered, in her disguised voice. "We're three—I mean, we're two freaks looking for work."

The door opened with a creak, and the children got their first look at Madame Lulu. She was wearing a long, shimmering robe that seemed to change colors as she moved, and a turban that looked very much like the one Count Olaf had worn back at Prufrock Preparatory School. She had dark, piercing eyes, with two dramatic eyebrows hovering suspiciously as she looked them over. Behind her, sitting at a small round table, were Count Olaf, Esmé Squalor, and Olaf's comrades, who were all staring at the youngsters curiously. And as if all those curious eyes weren't enough, there was one more eye gazing at the Baudelaires—a glass eye, attached to a chain around Madame Lulu's neck. The eye matched the one painted on her caravan, and the one tattooed on Count Olaf's ankle. It was an eye that seemed to follow the Baudelaires wherever they went, drawing them deeper and deeper into the troubling mystery of their lives.

"Walk in, please," Madame Lulu said in her strange accent, and the disguised children obeyed. As freakishly as they could, the Baudelaire orphans walked in, taking a few steps closer to all those staring eyes, and a few steps further from the lives they were leaving behind.

CHAPTER Three

Besides getting several paper cuts in the same day or receiving the news that someone in your family has betrayed you to your enemies, one of the most unpleasant experiences in life is a job interview. It is very nerve-wracking to explain to someone all the things you can do in the hopes that they will pay you to do them. I once had a very difficult job interview in which I had not only to explain that I could hit an olive with a bow and arrow, memorize up to three pages of poetry, and determine if there was poison mixed into cheese fondue without tasting it, but I had to demonstrate all these things as well. In most cases, the best strategy for a job interview is to be fairly honest, because the worst thing that can happen is that you won't get the job and will spend the rest of your life foraging for food in the wilderness and seeking shelter underneath a tree or the awning of a bowling alley that has gone out of business, but in the case of the Baudelaire orphans' job interview with Madame Lulu, the situation was much more desperate. They could not be honest at all, because they were disguised as entirely different people, and the worst thing that could happen was being discovered by Count Olaf and his troupe and spending the rest of their lives in circumstances so terrible that the children could not bear to think of them.

"Sit down, please, and Lulu will interview you for carnival job," Madame Lulu said, gesturing to the round table where Olaf and his troupe were sitting. Violet and Klaus sat down on one chair with difficulty, and Sunny crawled onto another while everyone watched them in silence. The troupe had their elbows on the table and were eating the snacks Lulu had provided with their fingers, while Esmé Squalor sipped her buttermilk, and Count Olaf leaned back in his chair and looked at the Baudelaires very, very carefully.

"It seems to me you look very familiar," he said.

"Perhaps you have seen before the freaks, my Olaf," Lulu said. "What are names of the freaks?"

"My name is Beverly," Violet said, in her low, disguised voice, inventing a name as quickly as she could invent an ironing board. "And this is my other head, Elliot."

Olaf reached across the table to shake hands, and Violet and Klaus had to stop for a moment to figure out whose arm was sticking out of the right-hand sleeve. "It's very nice to meet you

A SERIES OF UNFORTUNATE EVENTS

both," he said. "It must be very difficult, having two heads."

"Oh, yes," Klaus said, in as high a voice as he could manage. "You can't imagine how troublesome it is to find clothing."

"I was just noticing your shirt," Esmé said. "It's very in."

"Just because we're freaks," Violet said, "doesn't mean we don't care about fashion."

"How about eating?" Count Olaf said, his eyes shining brightly. "Do you have trouble eating?"

"Well, I—I mean, well, we—" Klaus said, but before he could go on, Olaf grabbed a long ear of corn from a platter on the table and held it toward the two children.

"Let's see how much trouble you have," he snarled, as his henchmen began to giggle. "Eat this ear of corn, you two-headed freak."

"Yes," Madame Lulu agreed. "It is best way to see if you can work in carnival. Eat corn! Eat corn!"

Violet and Klaus looked at one another, and then reached out one hand each to take the corn from Olaf and hold it awkwardly in front of their mouths. Violet leaned forward to take the first bite, but the motion of the corn made it slip from Klaus's hand and fall back down onto the table, and the room roared with cruel laughter.

"Look at them!" one of the white-faced women laughed. "They can't even eat an ear of corn! How freakish!"

"Try again," Olaf said with a nasty smile. "Pick the corn up from the table, freak."

The children picked up the corn and held it to their mouths once more. Klaus squinted and tried to take a bite, but when Violet tried to move the corn to help him, it hit him in the face and everyone—except for Sunny, of course—laughed once more.

"You are funny freaks," Madame Lulu said. She was laughing so hard that she had to wipe her eyes, and when she did, one of her dramatic eyebrows smeared slightly, as if she had a small bruise above one eye. "Try again, Beverly-and-Elliot freak!"

"This is the funniest thing I've ever seen," said the hook-handed man. "I always thought people with birth defects were unfortunate, but now I realize they're hilarious."

Violet and Klaus wanted to point out that a man with hooks for hands would probably have an equally difficult time eating an ear of corn, but they knew that a job interview is rarely a good time to start arguments, so the siblings swallowed their words and began swallowing corn. After a few bites, the children began to get their bearings, a phrase which here means "figure out how two people, using only two hands, can eat one ear of corn at the same time," but it was still quite a difficult task. The ear of corn was greasy with butter that left damp streaks on their mouths or dripped down their chins. Sometimes the ear of corn would be at a perfect angle for one of them to bite, but would be poking the other one in the face. And often the ear of corn

would simply slip out of their hands, and everyone would laugh yet again.

"This is more fun than kidnapping!" said
the bald associate of Olaf's, who was shaking
with laughter. "Lulu, this freak will have people
coming from miles around to watch, and all it
will cost you is an ear of corn!"

"Is true, please," Madame Lulu agreed, and
looked down at Violet and Klaus. "The crowd
loves sloppy eating," she said. "You are hired for
House of Freaks show."

"How about that other one?" Esmé asked,
giggling and wiping buttermilk from her upper
lip. "What is that freak, some sort of living scarf?"

"Chabo!" Sunny said to her siblings. She
meant something like, "I know this is humiliating, but at least our disguises are working!" but
Violet was quick to disguise her translation.

"This is Chabo the Wolf Baby," she said, in
her low voice. "Her mother was a hunter who
fell in love with a handsome wolf, and this is
their poor child."

"I didn't even know that was possible," said the hook-handed man.

"Grr," Sunny growled.

"It might be funny to watch her eat corn, too," said the bald man, and he grabbed another ear of corn and waved it at the youngest Baude-laire. "Here Chabo! Have an ear of corn!"

Sunny opened her mouth wide, but when the bald man saw the tips of her teeth poking out through the beard, he yanked his hand back in fear.

"Yikes!" he said. "That freak is vicious!"

"She's still a bit wild," Klaus said, still speaking as high as he could. "In fact, we got all these horrible scars from teasing her."

"Grr," Sunny growled again, and bit a piece of silverware to demonstrate how wild she was.

"Chabo will be excellent carnival attrac-tion," Madame Lulu pronounced. "People are always liking of violence, please. You are hired, too, Chabo."

"Just keep her away from me," Esmé said.

"A wolf baby like that would probably ruin my outfit."

"Grr!" Sunny growled.

"Come now, freaky people," Madame Lulu said. "Madame Lulu will show you the caravan, please, where you will do the sleeping."

"We'll stay here and have more wine," Count Olaf said. "Congratulations on the new freaks, Lulu. I knew you'd have good luck with me around."

"Everyone does," Esmé said, and kissed Olaf on the cheek. Madame Lulu scowled, and led the children out of her caravan and into the night.

"Follow me, freaks, please," she said. "You will be living, please, in freaks' caravan. You will share with other freaks. There is Hugo, Colette, and Kevin, all freaks. Every day will be House of Freaks show. Beverly and Elliot, you will be eating of corn, please. Chabo, you will be attacking of audience, please. Are there any freaky questions?"

"Will we be paid?" Klaus asked. He was thinking that having some money might help the Baudelaires, if they learned the answers to their questions and had an opportunity to get away from the carnival.

"No, no, no," Madame Lulu said. "Madame Lulu will be giving no money to the freaks, please. If you are freak, you are lucky that someone will give you work. Look at man with hooks on hands. He is grateful to do the working for Count Olaf, even though Olaf will not be giving him of the Baudelaire fortune."

"Count Olaf?" Violet asked, pretending that her worst enemy was a complete stranger. "Is that the gentleman with one eyebrow?"

"That is Olaf," Lulu said. "He is brilliant man, but do not be saying the wrong things to him, please. Madame Lulu always says you must always give people what they want, so always tell Olaf he is brilliant man."

"We'll remember that," Klaus said.

"Good, please," Madame Lulu said. "Now,

here is freak caravan. Welcome freaks, to your new home."

The fortune-teller had stopped at a caravan with the word FREAKS painted on it in large, sloppy letters. The letters were smeared and dripping in several places, as if the paint was still wet, but the word was so faded that the Baudelaires knew the caravan had been labeled many years ago. Next to the caravan was a shabby tent with several holes in it and a sign reading WELCOME TO THE HOUSE OF FREAKS, with a small drawing of a girl with three eyes. Madame Lulu strode past the sign to knock on the caravan's wooden door.

"Freaks!" Madame Lulu cried. "Please wake up, please! New freaks are here for you to say hello!"

"Just a minute, Madame Lulu," called a voice from behind the door.

"No just a minute, please," Madame Lulu said. "Now! I am the boss of the carnival!"

The door swung open to reveal a sleepy-looking man with a hunchback, a word which here means "a back with a hump near the shoulder, giving the person a somewhat irregular appearance." He was wearing a pair of pajamas that were ripped at the shoulder to make room for his hunchback, and holding a small candle to help him see in the dark. "I know you are the boss, Madame Lulu," the man said, "but it's the middle of the night. Don't you want your freaks to be well-rested?"

"Madame Lulu does not particularly care about sleep of freaks," Lulu said haughtily. "Please be telling the new freaks what to do for show tomorrow. The freak with two heads will be eating corn, please, and the little wolf freak will be attacking audience."

"Violence and sloppy eating," the man said, and sighed. "I guess the crowd will like that."

"Of course crowd will like," Lulu said, "and then carnival will get much money."

"And then maybe you'll pay us?" the man asked.

"Fat chance, please," Madame Lulu replied. "Good night, freaks."

"Good night, Madame Lulu," replied Violet, who would have rather been called a proper name, even if it was one she invented, than simply "freak," but the fortune-teller walked away without looking back. The Baudelaires stood in the doorway of the caravan for a moment, watching Lulu disappear into the night, before looking up at the man and introducing themselves a bit more properly.

"My name is Beverly," Violet said. "My second head is named Elliot, and this is Chabo the Wolf Baby."

"Grr!" growled Sunny.

"I'm Hugo," the man said. "It'll be nice to have new coworkers. Come on inside the caravan and I'll introduce you to the others."

Still finding it awkward to walk, Violet and Klaus followed Hugo inside, and Sunny followed her siblings, preferring to crawl rather than walk, because it made her seem more half wolf. The caravan was small, but the children could see by the light of Hugo's candle that it was tidy and clean. There was a small wooden table in the center, with a set of dominoes stacked up in the center and several chairs grouped around. In one corner was a rack with clothing hung on it, including a long row of identical coats, and a large mirror so you could comb your hair and make sure you looked presentable. There was a small stove for cooking meals, with a few pots and pans stacked alongside it, and a few potted plants lined up near the window so they would get enough sunlight. Violet would have liked to add a small workbench she could use while inventing things, Klaus would have been pleased to be squinting at some bookshelves, and Sunny would have preferred to see a stack of raw carrots or other foods that are pleasant to bite, but otherwise the caravan looked like a cozy place to live. The only thing that seemed to be missing was someplace to sleep, but as Hugo walked farther into the room, the children saw that there were three hammocks, which are long, wide pieces of cloth used for beds, hanging from places on the walls. One hammock was empty—the Baudelaires supposed that this was where Hugo slept—but in another they could see a tall skinny woman with curly hair squinting down at them, and in the third was a man with a very wrinkled face who was still asleep.

"Kevin!" Hugo called up to the sleeping man. "Kevin, get up! We have new coworkers, and I'll need help setting up more hammocks."

The man frowned and glared down at Hugo. "I wish you hadn't woken me up," Kevin said. "I was having a delightful dream that there was nothing wrong with me at all, instead of being a freak."

The Baudelaires took a good look at Kevin as he lowered himself to the floor and were unable to see anything the least bit freakish about him, but he stared at the Baudelaires as if he had seen a ghost. "My word," he said. "You two have it as bad as I do."

"Try to be polite, Kevin," Hugo said. "This is Beverly and Elliot, and there on the floor is Chabo the Wolf Baby."

"Wolf Baby?" Kevin repeated, shaking Violet and Klaus's shared right hand. "Is she dangerous?"

"She doesn't like to be teased," Violet said.

"I don't like to be teased either," Kevin said, and hung his head. "But wherever I go, I hear people whispering, 'there goes Kevin, the ambidextrous freak.'"

"Ambidextrous?" Klaus said. "Doesn't that mean you are both right-handed and left-handed?"

"So you've heard of me," Kevin said. "Is that why you traveled out here to the hinterlands, so you could stare at somebody who can write his name with either his left hand or his right?"

"No," Klaus said. "I just know the word 'ambidextrous' from a book I read."

"I had a feeling you'd be smart," Hugo said. "After all, you have twice as many brains as most people."

"I only have one brain," Kevin said sadly. "One brain, two ambidextrous arms, and two ambidextrous legs. What a freak!"

"It's better than being a hunchback," Hugo said. "Your hands may be freaky, but you have absolutely normal shoulders."

"What good are normal shoulders," Kevin said, "when they're attached to hands that are equally good at using a knife and fork?"

"Oh, Kevin," the woman said, and climbed down from her hammock to give him a pat on the head. "I know it's depressing being so freakish, but try and look on the bright side. At least you're better off than me." She turned to the children and gave them a shy smile. "My name is Colette," she said, "and if you're going to laugh at me, I'd prefer you do it now and get it over with."

The Baudelaires looked at Colette and then

at one another. "Renuf!" Sunny said, which meant something like, "I don't see anything freakish about you either, but even if I did I wouldn't laugh at you because it wouldn't be polite."

"I bet that's some sort of wolf laugh," Colette said, "but I don't blame Chabo for laughing at a contortionist."

"Contortionist?" Violet asked.

"Yes," Colette sighed. "I can bend my body into all sorts of unusual positions. Look."

The Baudelaires watched as Colette sighed again and launched into a contortionist routine. First she bent down so her head was between her legs, and curled up into a tiny ball on the floor. Then she pushed one hand against the ground and lifted her entire body up on just a few fingers, braiding her legs together into a spiral. Finally she flipped up in the air, balanced for a moment on her head, and twisted her arms and legs together like a mass of twine before looking up at the Baudelaires with a sad frown.

"You see?" Colette said. "I'm a complete freak."

"Wow!" Sunny shrieked.

"I thought that was amazing," Violet said, "and so did Chabo."

"That's very polite of you to say so," Colette said, "but I'm ashamed that I'm a contortionist."

"But if you're ashamed of it," Klaus said, "why don't you just move your body normally, instead of doing contortions?"

"Because I'm in the House of Freaks, Elliot," Colette said. "Nobody would pay to see me move my body normally."

"It's an interesting dilemma," Hugo said, using a fancy word for "problem" that the Baudelaires had learned from a law book in Justice Strauss's library. "All three of us would rather be normal people than freaks, but tomorrow morning, people will be waiting in the tent for Colette to twist her body into strange positions, for Beverly and Elliot to eat corn, for Chabo to growl and attack the crowd, for Kevin to write his name with both hands, and for me to try on one of those coats. Madame Lulu says we must always give people what they want, and they want freaks performing on a stage. Come now, it's very late at night. Kevin, give me a helping hand putting up hammocks for the newcomers, and then let's all try to get some sleep."

"I might as well give you *two* helping hands," Kevin said glumly. "They're both equally efficient. Oh, I wish that I was either right-handed or left-handed."

"Try to cheer up," Colette said gently. "Maybe a miracle will happen tomorrow, and we'll all get the things we wish for most."

No one in the caravan said anything more, but as Hugo and Kevin prepared two hammocks for the three Baudelaires, the children thought about what Colette had said. Miracles are like meatballs, because nobody can exactly agree what they are made of, where they come from, or how often they should appear. Some people say that a sunrise is a miracle, because it is some-what mysterious and often very beautiful, but other people say it is simply a fact of life, because it happens every day and far too early in the morning. Some people say that a telephone is a miracle, because it sometimes seems wondrous that you can talk with somebody who is thou-sands of miles away, and other people say it is simply a manufactured device fashioned out of metal parts, electronic circuitry, and wires that are very easily cut. And some people say that sneak-ing out of a hotel is a miracle, particularly if the lobby is swarming with policemen, and other people say it is simply a fact of life, because it happens every day and far too early in the morn-ing. So you might think that there are so many miracles in the world that you can scarcely count them, or that there are so few that they're scarcely worth mentioning, depending on whether you spend your mornings gazing at a beautiful sunset or lowering yourself into a back alley with a rope fashioned out of matching towels.

But there was one miracle the Baudelaires were thinking about as they lay in their hammocks and tried to sleep, and this was the sort of miracle that felt bigger than any meatball the world has ever seen. The hammocks creaked in the caravan as Violet and Klaus tried to get comfortable in one set of clothing and Sunny tried to arrange Olaf's beard so that it wouldn't be too scratchy, and all three youngsters thought about a miracle so wondrous and beautiful that it made their hearts ache to think of it. The miracle, of course, was that one of their parents was alive after all, that either their father or their mother had somehow survived the fire that had destroyed their home and begun the children's unfortunate journey. To have one more Baudelaire alive was such an enormous and unlikely miracle that the children were almost afraid to wish for it, but they wished for it anyway. The youngsters thought of what Colette had said—that maybe a miracle would happen, and that they would all get the thing they wished for most—and waited for morning to come, when Madame Lulu's crystal ball might bring the miracle the Baudelaires were wishing for.

At last the sun rose, as it does every day, and very early in the morning. The three children had slept very little and wished very much, and now they watched the caravan slowly fill with light, and listened to Hugo, Colette, and Kevin shift in their hammocks, and wondered if Count Olaf had entered the fortune-teller's tent yet, and if he had learned anything there. And just when they could stand it no more, they heard the sound of hurrying footsteps and a loud, metallic knock on the door.

"Wake up! Wake up!" came the voice of the hook-handed man, but before I write down what he said I must tell you that there is one more similarity between a miracle and a meatball, and it is that they both might appear to be one thing but turn out to be another. It happened to me once at a cafeteria, when it turned out there was a small camera hidden in the lunch

I received. And it happened to Violet, Klaus, and Sunny now, although it was quite some time before they learned that what the hook-handed man said turned out to be something different from what they thought when they heard him outside the door of the freaks' caravan.

"Wake up!" the hook-handed man said again, and pounded on the door. "Wake up and hurry up! I'm in a very bad mood and have no time for your nonsense. It's a very busy day at the carnival. Madame Lulu and Count Olaf are running errands, I'm in charge of the House of Freaks, the crystal ball revealed that one of those blasted Baudelaire parents is still alive, and the gift caravan is almost out of figurines."

CHAPTER Four

"What?" asked Hugo, yawning and rubbing his eyes. "What did you say?"

"I said the gift caravan is almost out of figurines," the hook-handed man said from behind the door. "But that's not your concern. People are already arriving at the carnival, so you freaks need to be ready in fifteen minutes."

"Wait a moment, sir!" Violet thought to use

her low, disguised voice just in time, as she and her brother climbed down from their hammock, still sharing a single pair of pants. Sunny was already on the floor, too astonished to remember to growl. "Did you say that one of the Baudelaire parents is alive?"

The door of the caravan opened a crack, and the children could see the face of the hook-handed man peering at them suspiciously.

"What do you care, freaks?" he asked.

"Well," Klaus said, thinking quickly, "we've been reading about the Baudelaires in *The Daily Punctilio*. We're very interested in the case of those three murderous children."

"Well," the hook-handed man said, "those kids' parents were supposed to be dead, but Madame Lulu looked into her crystal ball and saw that one of them was alive. It's a long story, but it means that we're all going to be very busy. Count Olaf and Madame Lulu had to leave early this morning to run an important errand, so I'm now in charge of the House of Freaks. That means I get to boss you around, so hurry up and get ready for the show!"

"Grr!" Sunny growled.

"Chabo's all set to perform," Violet said, "and the rest of us will be ready soon."

"You'd better be," the hook-handed man said, and began to shut the door before stopping for a moment. "That's funny," he said. "It looks like one of your scars is blurry."

"They blur as they heal," Klaus said.

"Too bad," the hook-handed man said. "It makes you look less freakish." He slammed the door and the siblings could hear him walk away from the caravan.

"I feel sorry for that man," Colette re-marked, as she swung down from her hammock and curled into a contortion on the floor. "Every time he and that Count person come to visit, it makes me feel bad to look at his hooks."

"He's better off than me," Kevin said, yawn-ing and stretching his ambidextrous arms. "At least one of his hooks is stronger than the other one. My arms and legs are exactly alike."

"And mine are very bendable," Colette said. "Well, we'd better do as the man says and get ready for the show."

"That's right," Hugo agreed, reaching into a shelf next to his hammock and pulling out a toothbrush. "Madame Lulu says that we must always give people what they want, and that man wants us ready right away."

"Here, Chabo," Violet said, looking down at her sister. "I'll help you sharpen your teeth."

"Grr!" Sunny agreed, and the two older Baudelaires leaned down together, and lifted Sunny up and moved into a corner so the three children could whisper to one another near the mirror, while Hugo, Colette, and Kevin performed their toilette, a phrase which here means "did the things necessary to begin their day as carnival freaks."

"What do you think?" Klaus asked. "Do you think it's really possible that one of our parents is alive?"

"I don't know," Violet said. "On one hand, it's hard to believe that Madame Lulu really has a magical crystal ball. On the other hand, she always told Count Olaf where we were so he could come and find us. I don't know what to believe."

"Tent," Sunny whispered.

"I think you're right, Sunny," Klaus said. "If we could sneak into the fortune-telling tent, we might be able to find out something for ourselves."

"You're whispering about me, aren't you?" Kevin called out from the other end of the caravan. "I bet you're saying, 'What a freak Kevin is. Sometimes he shaves with his left hand, and sometimes he shaves with his right hand, but it doesn't matter because they're *exactly the same*!'"

"We weren't talking about you, Kevin," Violet said. "We were discussing the Baudelaire case."

"I never heard of these Baudelaires," Hugo said, combing his hair. "Did I hear you mention they were murderers?"

"That's what it says in *The Daily Punctilio*," Klaus said.

"Oh, I never read the newspaper," Kevin said. "Holding it in both of my equally strong hands makes me feel like a freak."

"That's better than me," Colette said. "I can contort myself into a position that allows me to pick up a newspaper with my tongue. Talk about freakish!"

"It's an interesting dilemma," Hugo said, grabbing one of the identical coats from the rack, "but I think that we're all equally freakish. Now, let's get out there and put on a good show!"

The Baudelaires followed their coworkers out of the caravan and over to the House of Freaks tent, where the hook-handed man was standing impatiently, holding something long and damp in one of his hooks.

"Get inside and put on a good show," he ordered, gesturing to a flap in the tent that served as an entrance. "Madame Lulu said that if you don't give the audience what they want, I'm allowed to use this tagliatelle grande."

"What's a tagliatelle grande?" Colette asked.

"Tagliatelle is a type of Italian noodle," the hook-handed man explained, uncoiling the long and damp object, "and grande means 'big' in Italian. This is a big noodle that a carnival worker cooked up for me this morning." Olaf's comrade waved the big noodle over his head, and the Baudelaires and their coworkers heard a limp swishing sound as it moved slowly through the air, as if a large earthworm were crawling nearby. "If you don't do what I say," the hook-handed man continued, "I get to hit you with the tagliatelle grande, which I've heard is an unpleasant and somewhat sticky experience."

"Don't worry, sir," Hugo said. "We're professionals."

"I'm glad to hear it," the hook-handed man sneered, and followed them all into the House of Freaks. Inside, the tent looked even bigger, particularly because there wasn't very much to see in such a large space. There was a wooden stage with a few folding chairs placed on it, and a banner overhead, which read HOUSE OF FREAKS in large, sloppy letters. There was a small stand where one of the white-faced women was selling cold beverages. And there were seven or eight people milling around, waiting for the show to begin. Madame Lulu had mentioned that business had been slow at Caligari Carnival, but the siblings had still expected a few more people to show up to see the carnival freaks. As the children and their co-workers approached the stage, the hook-handed man began speaking to the small group of people as if they were a vast crowd.

"Ladies and gentlemen, boys and girls, adolescents of both genders," he announced. "Hurry up and buy your delicious cold beverages, because the House of Freaks show is about to begin!"

"Look at all those freaks!" giggled one

member of the audience, a middle-aged man with several large pimples on his chin. "There's a man with hooks instead of hands!"

"I'm not one of the freaks," the hook-handed man growled. "I work here at the carnival!"

"Oh, I'm sorry," the man said. "But if you don't mind my saying so, if you purchased a pair of realistic hands no one would make that mistake."

"It's not polite to comment on other people's appearances," the hook-handed man said sternly. "Now, ladies and gentlemen, gaze with horror on Hugo, the hunchback! Instead of a regular back, he has a big hump that makes him look very freakish!"

"That's true," said the pimpled man, who seemed willing to giggle at one person or another. "What a freak!"

The hook-handed man waved his large noodle in the air as a limp reminder to the Baudelaires and their coworkers. "Hugo!" he barked. "Put on your coat!"

As the audience tittered, Hugo walked to the front of the stage and tried to put on the coat he was holding. Usually, if someone has a body with an unusual shape, they will hire a tailor to alter their clothing so it will fit comfortably and attractively, but as Hugo struggled with the coat, it was clear that no such tailor had been hired. Hugo's hump wrinkled the back of the coat, and then stretched it, and then finally ripped it as he did up the buttons, so that within moments the coat was just a few pieces of tattered cloth. Blushing, Hugo retreated to the back of the stage and sat on a folding chair as the members of the tiny audience howled with laughter.

"Isn't that hilarious?" the hook-handed man said. "He can't even put on a coat! What a freakish person! But wait, ladies and gentlemen—there's more!" Olaf's henchman shook the tagliatelle grande again while reaching into his pocket with his other hook. Smiling wickedly, he withdrew an ear of corn and held it up for the audience to see. "This is a simple ear of corn," he announced. "It's something that any normal person can eat. But here at Caligari Carnival, we don't have a House of Normal People. We have a House of Freaks, with a brand-new freak that will turn this ear of corn into a hilarious mess!"

Violet and Klaus sighed, and walked to the center of the stage, and I do not think that I have to describe this tiresome show any longer. You can undoubtedly guess that the two eldest Baudelaires were forced to eat another ear of corn while a small group of people laughed at them, and that Colette was forced to twist her body into unusual shapes and positions, and that Kevin had to write his name with both his left and right hands, and that finally poor Sunny was forced to growl at the audience, although she was not a ferocious person by nature and would have preferred to greet them politely. And you can imagine how the crowd reacted as the hook-handed man announced each person and forced them to do these things. The seven or eight people laughed, and shouted cruel names, and made terrible and tasteless jokes, and one woman even threw her cold beverage, paper cup and all, at Kevin, as if someone who was both right-handed and left-handed somehow deserved to have wet and sticky stains on his shirt. But what you may not be able to imagine, unless you have had a similar experience yourself, is how humiliating it was to participate in such a show. You might think that being humiliated, like riding a bicycle or decoding a secret message, would get easier after you had done it a few times, but the Baudelaires had been laughed at more than a few times and it didn't make their experience in the House of Freaks easier at all. Violet remembered when a girl named Carmelita Spats had laughed at her and called her names, when the children were enrolled in Prufrock Preparatory School, but it still hurt her feelings when the hook-handed man announced her as something hilarious. Klaus remembered when Esmé Squalor had insulted him at 667 Dark Avenue, but he still blushed when the audience pointed and giggled every time the ear of corn slipped out of his hands. And Sunny remembered all of the times Count Olaf had laughed at all three Baudelaires and their misfortune, but she still felt embarrassed and a little sick when the people called her "wolf freak" as she followed the other performers out of the tent when the show was over. The Baudelaire orphans even knew that they weren't really a two-headed person and a wolf baby, but as they sat with their coworkers in the freaks' caravan afterward, they felt so humiliated that it was as if they were as freakish as everyone thought.

"I don't like this place," Violet said to Kevin and Colette, sharing a chair with her brother at the caravan's table, while Hugo made hot chocolate at the stove. She was so upset that she almost forgot to speak in a low voice. "I don't like being stared at, and I don't like being laughed at. If people think it's funny when someone drops an ear of corn, they should stay home and drop it themselves."

"Kiwoon!" Sunny agreed, forgetting to growl. She meant something along the lines of, "I thought I was going to cry when all those people were calling me 'freak,'" but luckily only her siblings understood her, so she didn't give away her disguise.

"Don't worry," Klaus said to his sisters. "I don't think we'll stay here very long. The fortune-telling tent is closed today because Count Olaf and Madame Lulu are running that important errand." The middle Baudelaire did not need to add that it would be a good time to sneak into the tent and find out if Lulu's crystal ball really held the answers they were seeking.

"Why do you care if Lulu's tent is closed?" Colette asked. "You're a freak, not a fortune-teller."

"And why don't you want to stay here?" Kevin asked. "Caligari Carnival hasn't been very popular lately, but there's nowhere else for a freak to go."

"Of course there is," Violet said. "Lots of people are ambidextrous, Kevin. There are ambidextrous florists, and ambidextrous air-traffic controllers, and all sorts of things."

"You really think so?" Kevin asked.

"Of course I do," Violet said. "And it's the same with contortionists and hunchbacks. All of us could find some other type of job where people didn't think we were freakish at all."

"I'm not sure that's true," Hugo called over from the stove. "I think that a two-headed person is going to be considered pretty freakish no matter where they go."

"And it's probably the same with an ambidextrous person," Kevin said with a sigh.

"Let's try to forget our troubles and play dominoes," Hugo said, bringing over a tray with six steaming mugs of hot chocolate. "I thought both of your heads might want to drink separately," he explained with a smile, "particularly because this hot chocolate is a little bit unusual. Chabo the Wolf Baby added a little bit of cinnamon."

"Chabo added it?" Klaus asked with surprise, as Sunny growled modestly.

"Yes," Hugo said. "At first I thought it was some freaky wolf recipe, but it's actually quite tasty."

"That was a clever idea, Chabo," Klaus said, and gave his sister a squinty smile. It seemed only a little while ago that the youngest Baudelaire couldn't walk, and was small enough to fit inside a birdcage, and now she was developing her own interests, and was big enough to seem half wolf.

"You should be very proud of yourself," Hugo agreed. "If you weren't a freak, Chabo, you could grow up to be an excellent chef."

"She could be a chef anyway," Violet said. "Elliot, would you mind if we stepped outside to enjoy our hot chocolate?"

"That's a good idea," Klaus said quickly. "I've always considered hot chocolate to be an outdoor beverage, and I'd like to take a peek in the gift caravan."

"Grr," Sunny growled, but her siblings knew she meant "I'll come with you," and she crawled over to where Violet and Klaus were awkwardly rising from their chair.

"Don't be too long," Colette said. "We're not supposed to wander around the carnival."

"We'll just drink our hot chocolate and come right back," Klaus promised.

"I hope you don't get in trouble," Kevin said. "I hate to think of the tagliatelle grande hitting both of your heads."

The Baudelaires were just about to point out that a blow from the tagliatelle grande probably wouldn't hurt one bit, when they heard a noise which was far more fearsome than a large noodle waving in the air. Even from inside the caravan, the children could hear a loud, creaky noise they recognized from their long trip into the hinterlands.

"That sounds like that gentleman friend of Madame Lulu's," Hugo said. "That's the sound of his car."

"There's another sound, too," Colette said. "Listen."

The children listened and heard that the contortionist had spoken the truth. Accompanying the roar of the engine was another roar, one that sounded deeper and angrier than any automobile. The Baudelaires knew that you cannot judge something by its sound any more than you can judge a person by the way they look, but this roar was so loud and fierce that the youngsters could not imagine that it brought good news.

Here I must interrupt the story I am writing, and tell you another story in order to make an important point. This second story is fictional, a word which here means "somebody made it up one day," as opposed to the story of the Baudelaire orphans, which somebody merely wrote down, usually at night. It is called "The Story of Queen Debbie and Her Boyfriend, Tony," and it goes something like this:

The Story of Queen Debbie and Her Boyfriend, Tony

Once upon a time, there lived a fictional queen named Queen Debbie, who ruled over the land where this story takes place, which is made up. This fictional land had lollipop trees growing everywhere, and singing mice that did all of the chores, and there were fierce and fictional lions who guarded the palace against fictional enemies. Queen Debbie had a boyfriend named Tony, who lived in the neighboring fictional kingdom. Because they lived so far away, Debbie and Tony couldn't see each other that often, but occasionally they would go out to dinner and a movie, or do other fictional things together.

Tony's birthday arrived, and Queen Debbie had some royal business and couldn't travel to see him, but she sent him a nice card and a myna bird in a shiny cage. The proper thing to do if you receive a present, of course, is to write a thank-you note, but Tony was not a particularly proper person, and called Debbie to complain.

"Debbie, this is Tony," Tony said. "I got the birthday present you sent me, and I don't like it at all."

"I'm sorry to hear that," Queen Debbie said, plucking a lollipop off a nearby tree. "I picked out the myna bird especially for you. What sort of present would you prefer?"

"I think you should give me a bunch of valuable diamonds," said Tony, who was as greedy as he was fictional.

"Diamonds?" Queen Debbie said. "But myna birds can cheer you up when you are sad. You can teach them to sit on your hand, and sometimes they even talk."

"I want diamonds," Tony said.

"But diamonds are so valuable," Queen Debbie

said. "If I send you diamonds in the mail, they'll probably get stolen on their way to you, and then you won't have any birthday present at all."

"I want diamonds," whined Tony, who was really becoming quite tiresome.

"I know what I'll do," Queen Debbie said with a faint smile. "I'll feed my diamonds to the royal lions, and then send the lions to your kingdom. No one would dare attack a bunch of fierce lions, so the diamonds are sure to arrive safely."

"Hurry up," Tony said. "It's supposed to be my special day."

It was easy for Queen Debbie to hurry up, because the singing mice who lived in her palace did all of the necessary chores, so it only took a few minutes for her to feed a bunch of diamonds to her lions, wrapping the jewels in tuna fish first so the lions would agree to eat them. Then she instructed the lions to travel to the neighboring kingdom to deliver the present.

Tony waited impatiently outside his house for the rest of the day, eating all of the ice cream and cake and teasing his myna bird, and finally, at just about sunset, he saw the lions approaching on the horizon and ran over to collect his present.

"Give me those diamonds, you stupid lions!" Tony cried, and there is no need to tell you the rest of this story, which has the rather obvious moral "Never look a gift lion in the mouth." The point is that there are times where the arrival of a bunch of lions is good news, particularly in a fictional story where the lions are not real and so probably will not hurt you. There are some cases, as in the case of Queen Debbie and her boyfriend, Tony, where the arrival of lions means that the story is about to get much better.

But I am sad to say that the case of the Baudelaire orphans is not one of those times. The story of the Baudelaires does not take place in a fictional land where lollipops grow on trees and singing mice do all of the chores. The story of the Baudelaires takes place in a very real world, where some people are laughed at just because they have something wrong with them, and where children can find themselves all alone in the world, struggling to understand the sinister mystery that surrounds them, and in this real world the arrival of lions means that the story is about to get much worse, and if you do not have a stomach for such a story—any more than lions have a stomach for diamonds not coated in tuna fish—it would be best if you turned around right now and ran the other way, as the Baudelaires wished they could as they exited the caravan and saw what Count Olaf had brought with him when he returned from his errand.

Count Olaf drove his black automobile between the rows of caravans, nearly running over several visitors to the carnival, stopped right at the tent for the House of Freaks, and turned off the engine, which ended the creaky roar the children had recognized. But the other, angrier roar continued as Olaf got out of the car, followed by Madame Lulu, and pointed with a flourish to a trailer that was attached to the rear of the automobile. The trailer was really more of a metal cage on wheels, and through the bars of the cage the Baudelaires could see what the villain was pointing at.

The trailer was filled with lions, packed in so tightly that the children couldn't tell just how many there were. The lions were unhappy to be traveling in such tight quarters, and were showing their unhappiness by scratching at the cage with their claws, snapping at one another with their long teeth, and roaring as loudly and as fiercely as they could. Some of Count Olaf's henchmen gathered around, along with several visitors to the carnival, to see what was going on, and Olaf tried to say something to them, but couldn't be heard over the lions' roars. Frowning, the villain removed a whip from his pocket and whipped at the lions through the trailer bars. Like people, animals will become frightened and likely do whatever you say if you whip them enough, and the lions finally quieted down so Olaf could make his announcement.

"Ladies and gentlemen," he said, "boys and girls, freaks and normal people, Caligari Carnival is proud to announce the arrival of these fierce lions, who will be used in a new attraction."

"That's good news," said someone in the crowd, "because the souvenirs in the gift caravan are pretty lousy."

"It *is* good news," Count Olaf agreed with a snarl, and turned to face the Baudelaires. His eyes were shining very brightly, and the siblings shivered in their disguises as he looked at the children and then at the gathering crowd. "Things are about to get much better around here," he said, and the Baudelaire orphans knew that this was as fictional as anything they could imagine.

If you have ever experienced something that feels strangely familiar, as if the exact same thing has happened to you before, then you are experiencing what the French call "déjà vu." Like most French expressions—"ennui," which is a fancy term for severe boredom, or "la petite mort," which describes a feeling that part of you has died—"déjà vu" refers to something that is usually not very pleasant, because it is curious to feel as if you have heard or seen something that you have heard or seen before.

If you have ever experienced something that feels strangely familiar, as if the exact same thing has happened to you before, then you are experiencing what the French call "déjà vu." Like most French expressions—"ennui," which is a fancy term for severe boredom, or "la petite mort," which describes a feeling that part of you has died—"déjà vu" refers to something that is usually not very pleasant, and it was not pleasant for the Baudelaire orphans to stand outside the freaks' caravan listening to Count Olaf and experiencing the queasy feeling of déjà vu.

"These lions are going to be the most excit-ing thing at Caligari Carnival!" Olaf announced, as more and more people drew near to see what all the fuss was about. "As you all know, unless you are incredibly dim-witted, a stubborn mule will move in the proper direction if there is a carrot in front of it, and a stick behind it. It will move toward the carrot, because it wants the reward of food, and away from the stick, because it does not want the punishment of pain. And these lions will do the same."

"What's going on?" Hugo asked the chil-dren, walking out of the caravan with Colette and Kevin close behind.

"Déjà vu," Sunny said bitterly. Even the youngest Baudelaire recognized Count Olaf's cruel speech about the stubborn mule from when the three children had been living in Olaf's house. Back then, the villain had talked about a stubborn mule in order to force Violet to marry him, a plot that thankfully had been foiled at the last minute, but now he was using the very same words to cook up another scheme, and it gave the siblings a queasy feeling to watch it happen.

"These lions," Count Olaf said, "will do as I say, because they want to avoid the punishment of this whip!" With a flourish, he flicked his whip at the lions again, who cowered behind the bars, and some of the visitors to the carnival applauded.

"But if the whip is the stick," asked the bald man, "what is the carrot?"

"The carrot?" Olaf repeated, and laughed in a particularly nasty way. "The reward for the lions who obey me will be a delicious meal. Lions are carnivorous, which means they eat meat, and here at Caligari Carnival they'll have the finest meat we have to offer." He turned and pointed his whip at the entrance to the freaks' caravan, where the Baudelaires were standing with their coworkers. "The freaks you see here aren't normal people, and so they lead depressing lives," he announced. "They'll be happy to exhibit themselves in the name of entertainment."

"Of course we will," Colette said. "We do it every day."

"Then you won't mind being the most important part of the lion show," Olaf replied. "We're not going to feed these lions regular meals, so they'll be very, very hungry by the time the show begins. Each day, instead of a show at the House of Freaks, we'll randomly choose one freak and watch the lions devour them."

Everyone cheered again, except for Hugo, Colette, Kevin, and the three siblings, who all stood in horrified silence.

"That will be exciting!" said the man with pimples on his face. "Just think—violence and sloppy eating combined in one fabulous show!"

"I couldn't agree more!" said a woman who was standing nearby. "It was hilarious watching that two-headed freak eat, but it'll be even more hilarious watching the two-headed freak get eaten!"

"I'd prefer to watch the hunchback get eaten," said someone else in the crowd. "He's so funny! He doesn't even have a regular back!"

"The fun starts tomorrow afternoon!" Count Olaf cried. "See you then!"

"I can't wait," said the woman, as the crowd began to disperse, a word which here means "walk off to purchase souvenirs or leave the carnival." "I'm going to tell all my friends."

"I'm going to call that reporter at *The Daily Punctilio*," the man with pimples said, heading toward the phone booth. "This carnival is about to get very popular, and maybe they'll write an article about it."

"You were right, boss," said the hook-handed man. "Things are about to get much better here."

"Of course he was right, please," Madame Lulu said. "He is brilliant man, and brave man, and generous man. He is brilliant for thinking of the lion show, please. He is brave man for hitting lions with whip, please. And he is generous man for giving lions to Lulu."

"He gave those lions to you?" asked a sinister voice. "They were presents?"

Now that most of the carnival visitors had departed, the Baudelaires could see Esmé Squalor step forward from the doorway of another caravan and walk toward Count Olaf and Madame Lulu. As she passed the lions' trailer, she ran her enormous fingernails along the bars, and the lions whimpered in fear. "So you gave Madame Lulu some lions," she said. "What did you get me?"

Count Olaf scratched his head with one scraggly hand, and looked a little embarrassed. "Nothing," he admitted. "But you can share my whip, if you'd like."

Madame Lulu leaned over and gave Olaf a kiss on the cheek. "He gave lions to me, please, because I did such wonderful fortune-telling."

"You should have seen it, Esmé," Olaf said.

"Lulu and I entered the fortune-telling tent and turned out all the lights, and the crystal ball began to hum its magical hum. Then, magical lightning crackled above us, and Madame Lulu told me to concentrate as hard as I could. While I closed my eyes, she gazed into her crystal ball and told me that one of the Baudelaire parents is alive and hiding in the Mortmain Mountains. As a reward, I gave her these lions."

"So Madame Lulu needs a carrot, too, eh?" the hook-handed man said with a laugh.

"First thing tomorrow morning," Olaf continued, "Madame Lulu will consult her crystal ball again, and tell me where the Baudelaires are."

Esmé glared at Lulu. "And what sort of gift will you give then, Olaf?"

"Be reasonable, my dear," Count Olaf said to his girlfriend. "The lions will make Caligari Carnival much more popular, so Madame Lulu can devote her time to fortune-telling and give us the information we need to finally steal the

Baudelaire fortune."

"I hate to criticize," Hugo said hesitantly, "but is there any way we can make the carnival more popular without feeding us to the lions? I must confess that I'm a little nervous about that part."

"You heard the crowd when I told them about the new attraction," Count Olaf said. "They couldn't wait to see the lions devour you, and all of us need to do our part to give people what they want. Your part is to return to the freaks' caravan until tomorrow. And the rest of us will do our part and start digging the pit."

"Pit?" one of the white-faced women asked. "What do we need a pit for?"

"To keep the lions in," Olaf replied, "so they only eat whichever freak jumps down there. Let's dig it over by the roller coaster."

"Good idea, boss," the bald man said.

"There are shovels in tool caravan," Lulu said. "I will show you, please."

"I'm not going to dig a pit," Esmé announced

as the others walked away. "I might break a nail. Besides, I need to talk to Count Olaf—*alone*."

"Oh, all right," Count Olaf said. "Let's go in the guest caravan where we won't be disturbed."

Olaf and Esmé walked off in one direction, and Madame Lulu led the henchmen in the other, leaving the three children alone with their coworkers.

"Well, we'd better go inside," Colette said. "Maybe we can think of a way not to get eaten."

"Oh, let's not think about those fearsome creatures," Hugo said with a shudder. "Let's play another game of dominoes instead."

"Chabo, my other head, and I will be along in a moment," Violet said. "We want to finish our hot chocolate."

"You might as well enjoy it," Kevin said glumly, following Hugo and Colette back into the freaks' caravan. "It might turn out to be the last hot chocolate you ever drink."

Kevin shut the door with both hands, and the Baudelaires stepped farther away from the caravan so they could talk without being over-heard.

"Adding cinnamon to hot chocolate is a ter-rific idea, Sunny," Violet said, "but I'm having trouble enjoying it."

"Ificat," Sunny said, which meant "Me too."

"Count Olaf's latest scheme leaves a bad taste in my mouth," Klaus said, "and I don't think cinnamon will help."

"We have to get into that fortune-telling tent," Violet said, "and this may be our only chance."

"Do you think it's really true?" Klaus asked. "Do you think Madame Lulu really saw some-thing in her crystal ball?"

"I don't know," Violet said, "but I do know from my studies of electricity that lightning can't appear inside a tent. Something mysteri-ous is going on, and we need to find out what it is."

"Chow!" Sunny said, which meant "Before we're thrown to the lions!"

"But do you think it's real?" Klaus asked.

"I don't know," Violet said testily, a word which here means "in her regular voice, forgetting her disguise because she was becoming very frustrated and upset." "I don't know if Madame Lulu is a fortune-teller. I don't know how Count Olaf always knows where we are. I don't know where the Snicket file is, or why someone else had Olaf's tattoo, or what V.F.D. stands for, or why there's a secret passageway that leads to our house, or—"

"If our parents are alive?" Klaus interrupted. "Do you know if one of our parents is really alive?"

The middle Baudelaire's voice quivered, and his sisters turned to look at him—a feat that was difficult for Violet, who was still sharing his shirt—and saw that he was crying. Violet leaned so that her head was against his while Sunny put her mug down and crawled closer to hug his knees, and the three Baudelaires stood quietly together for a few moments.

Grief, a type of sadness that most often occurs when you have lost someone you love, is a sneaky thing, because it can disappear for a long time, and then pop back up when you least expect it. When I am able, I go out walking on Briny Beach very early in the morning, which is the best time to find materials important to the Baudelaire case, and the ocean is so peaceful that I feel peaceful, too, as if I am no longer grieving for the woman I love and will never see again. But then, when I am cold and duck into a teashop where the owner is expecting me, I have only to reach for the sugar bowl before my grief returns, and I find myself crying so loudly that other customers ask me if I could possibly lower my sobs. With the Baudelaire orphans, it was as if their grief were a very heavy object that they each took turns carrying so that they would not all be crying at once, but sometimes the object was too heavy for one of them to move without weeping, so Violet and Sunny stood next to Klaus, reminding him that this was something they could all carry together until at last they found a safe place to lay it down.

"I'm sorry I was testy, Klaus," Violet said. "There's just so much we don't know that it's hard to think about all at once."

"Chithvee," Sunny said, which meant "But I can't help thinking about our parents."

"Me neither," Violet admitted. "I keep wondering if one of them survived the fire."

"But if they did," Klaus said, "why would they be hiding in a faraway place? Why aren't they trying to find us?"

"Maybe they are," Violet said quietly. "Maybe they're searching for us everywhere they can think of, but they can't find us, because we've been hiding and disguising ourselves for so long."

"But why doesn't our mother or father contact Mr. Poe?" Klaus said.

"We've tried to contact him," Violet pointed out, "but he doesn't answer our telegrams, and we can't seem to reach him by phone. If one of our parents has survived the fire, maybe they're having the same wretched luck."

"Galfuskin," Sunny pointed out. By "Galfuskin" she meant something like, "This is all guesswork—let's go to the fortune-telling tent and see if we can find out anything for sure, and we'd better do it soon before the others get back."

"You're right, Sunny," Violet said, and put her mug down next to Sunny's. Klaus put down his mug, and all three Baudelaires took disguised steps away from their hot chocolate. Violet and Klaus walked awkwardly in their shared pants, leaning against one another with every step, and Sunny followed alongside, still crawling so that she would look half wolf if anyone watched them as they made their way through the carnival toward the fortune-telling tent. But no one was watching the Baudelaire orphans. The visitors to the carnival had gone home to tell their friends about the lion show happening the next day. The children's coworkers were in the freaks' caravan bemoaning their fate, a word which here means "playing dominoes, rather than trying to think of a way out of their predicament." Madame Lulu and Olaf's assistants were digging the pit, over by the roller coaster still covered in ivy. Count Olaf and Esmé Squalor were bickering in the guest caravan, which was located at the far end of the carnival where I had stayed with my brother so many years ago, and the rest of Madame Lulu's employees were closing down the carnival and hoping that someday they might work in a less miserable place. So nobody was watching as the children approached the tent next to Lulu's caravan, and stopped for a minute at the flap that led inside.

The fortune-telling tent no longer stands at Caligari Carnival, or anywhere else for that matter. Anyone wandering through the blackened and desolate hinterlands would scarcely be able to tell that there had been any tents at all. But even if everything looked exactly the same as when the Baudelaire orphans stayed there, it is unlikely that a traveler would understand what the tent's decoration meant, as nowadays there are so few living experts on such subjects, and the experts who are alive are all in terrible circumstances, or, in my case, on their way to terrible circumstances in the hopes of making them less terrible. But the Baudelaire orphans— who, as you will recall, had only arrived at the carnival the night before, and so had never seen the fortune-telling tent in daylight until this very moment—could see how the tent was decorated, which is why they stopped to stare at it.

At first glance, the painting on the fortune-telling tent seemed to depict an eye, like the decoration on Madame Lulu's caravan and the tattoo on Count Olaf's ankle. The three children had seen similar eyes wherever they went, from a building in the shape of an eye when they were working in a lumbermill, to an eye on Esmé Squalor's purse when they were hiding in a hospital, to a huge swarm of eyes that surrounded them in their most frightening nightmares, and although the siblings never understood quite what these eyes meant, they were so weary of gazing at them that they would never pause to look at one again. But there are many things in life that become different if you take a long look at them, and as the children paused in front of the fortune-telling tent, the painting seemed to change before their very eyes, until it did not seem like a painting at all, but an insignia.

An insignia is sort of a mark that usually stands for an organization or a business, and the mark can be of any sort whatsoever. Sometimes an insignia can be a simple shape, such as a wavy line to indicate an organization concerned with rivers or oceans, or a square to indicate an organization concerned with geometry or sugar cubes. Sometimes an insignia can be a small picture of something, such as a torch, to indicate an organization that is flammable, or the three-eyed girl outside the House of Freaks, indicating that people who were unusual in some way were on display inside. And sometimes an insignia can be part of the name of the organization, such as the first few letters, or its initials. The Baudelaires, of course, were not involved in any sort of business, aside from disguising themselves as carnival freaks, and as far as they knew they were not members of an organization of any kind, and they had never even been to the hinterlands until Count Olaf's car had taken them down Rarely Ridden Road, but the three children took a long look at the insignia on Madame Lulu's tent, because they knew that it was important to them somehow, as if whoever had painted the insignia knew they would come here, and wanted to bring them inside.

"Do you think . . ." Klaus said, his voice trailing off as he squinted at the tent.

"I didn't see it at first glance," Violet said, "but as I took a long look . . ."

"Volu . . ." Sunny said, and without another word the three children peered into the entrance, and, seeing no sign of anyone inside, took a few steps forward. If someone had been watching the youngsters, they would have seen these few hesitant steps as they entered the fortune-teller's tent as quietly as they could. But there was no one watching. There was no one to see the flap of cloth as it closed quietly behind them, making the whole tent shiver ever so slightly, and there was no one to notice that the painting shivered, too. There was no one watching the Baudelaire orphans as they drew closer to finding the answers to their questions, or solving the mysteries of their lives. There was no one to take a long look at the painting on the tent to see that it was not an image of an eye, as it appeared to be at first glance, but an insignia, standing for an organization the children knew only as V.F.D.

CHAPTER

Six

There are many difficult things in this
world to hide, but a secret is not one of
them. It is difficult to hide an airplane,
for instance, because you generally
need to find a deep hole or an enormous haystack, and sneak the airplane
inside in the middle of the night, but
it is easy to hide a secret about an airplane, because you can merely write it
on a tiny piece of paper and tape it to

the bottom of your mattress any time you are at home. It is difficult to hide a symphony orchestra, because you usually need to rent a sound-proof room and borrow as many sleeping bags as you can find, but it is easy to hide a secret about a symphony orchestra, because you can merely whisper it into the ear of a trustworthy friend or music critic. And it is difficult to hide yourself, because you sometimes need to stuff yourself into the trunk of an automobile, or concoct a disguise out of whatever you can find, but it is easy to hide a secret about yourself, because you can merely type it into a book and hope it falls into the right hands. My dear sister, if you are reading this, I am still alive, and heading north to try and find you.

Had the Baudelaire orphans been looking for an airplane as they stepped inside Madame Lulu's fortune-telling tent, they would have known to look for the tip of a wing, sticking out from under an enormous black tablecloth decorated with shiny silver stars, which hung over a table in the center of the tent. Had they been looking for a symphony orchestra, they would have known to listen for the sound of someone coughing or bumping up against an oboe as they hid in the corners of the tent, which were covered in heavy curtains. But the children were not looking for methods of air travel or professional musicians. They were looking for secrets, and the tent was so big that they scarcely knew where to begin looking. Was there news of the Baudelaire parents hidden in the cupboard that stood near the entrance? Could there be information about the Snicket file stuffed into the large trunk that stood in one of the corners? And was it possible the children could find out the meaning of V.F.D. by gazing into the crystal ball placed in the center of the table? Violet, Klaus, and Sunny looked around the tent, and then at one another, and it seemed that the secrets concerning them could be hidden just about anywhere.

"Where do you think we should look?" Violet asked.

"I don't know," Klaus replied, squinting all around him. "I'm not even sure what to look for."

"Well, maybe we should look for answers the way Count Olaf did," Violet said. "He told the whole story of his fortune-telling experience."

"I remember," Klaus said. "First he entered Madame Lulu's tent. We've done that. Then, he said they turned out all the lights."

The Baudelaires looked up, and noticed for the first time that the ceiling of the tent was decorated with small lights in the shape of stars, matching the stars on the tablecloth.

"Switch!" Sunny said, pointing to a pair of switches attached to one of the tent poles.

"Good work, Sunny," Violet said. "Here, Klaus, walk with me so I can get a look at those switches."

The two older Baudelaires walked freakishly over to the pole, but when they reached the switches Violet frowned and shook her head.

"What's wrong?" Klaus asked.

"I wish I had a ribbon," Violet said, "to tie

up my hair. It's hard to think seriously with my powdery hair getting in my eyes. But my hair ribbon is somewhere at Heimlich. . . ."

Her voice trailed off, and Klaus saw that she had reached her hand into the pocket of Count Olaf's pants and was drawing out a ribbon that looked just like the one she usually wore.

"Yerz," Sunny said.

"It *is* mine," Violet said, looking at it closely. "Count Olaf must have kept it when he was preparing me for surgery, and left it in his pocket."

"I'm glad you got it back," Klaus said, with a slight shudder. "I don't like to think about Olaf getting his filthy hands on our possessions. Do you need some help tying your hair up? It might be difficult using only one hand, and I don't think you should take your other one out from under the shirt. We don't want to mess up our disguise."

"I think I can manage it with one hand," Violet said. "Ah, there we go. I feel less like a freak and more like Violet Baudelaire with my hair up like this. Now, let's see. Both these switches are attached to wires that run up to the top of the tent. One of them obviously controls the lights, but what does the other one do?"

The Baudelaires looked up again, and saw something else attached to the ceiling of the tent. In between the stars was a small, round mirror, hanging from a piece of metal, which held it at an odd angle. Attached to the metal was a long strip of rubber, which led to a large knot of wires and gears, which in turn was attached to some more mirrors arranged in a sort of wheel.

"What?" Sunny asked.

"I don't know," Klaus said. "It sure doesn't look like anything I've read about."

"It's an invention of some sort," Violet said, studying it carefully. She began to point to different parts of the strange device, but it was as if she were talking to herself instead of her siblings. "That piece of rubber looks like a fan belt, which transmits torque from an automotive engine in order to help cool the radiator. But why would you want to—oh, I see. It moves those other mirrors around, which—but how would—wait a minute. Klaus, see that small hole in the upper corner of the tent?"

"Not without my glasses," Klaus said.

"Well, there's a small rip up there," Violet said. "What direction are we facing, if we face that small hole?"

"Let me think for a moment," Klaus said. "Last night, the sun was setting as we got out of the car."

"Yirat," Sunny said, which meant "I remember—the famous hinterlands sunset."

"And the car is over there," Klaus said, turning around and dragging his older sister with them. "So that way is west, and the rip in the tent faces east."

"East," Violet said with a smile, "the direction of the sunrise."

"That's right," Klaus said, "but what does that have to do with anything?"

Violet said nothing, just stood and smiled at her siblings, and Klaus and Sunny smiled back. Even with the fake scars penciled on her face, Violet was smiling in a way the other Baudelaires recognized at once. It was the sort of smile that appeared when Violet had figured out a difficult problem, usually having to do with an invention of some sort. She had smiled this way when the siblings were in jail, and she figured out how a pitcher of water could help break them out. She had smiled this way when she had looked over some evidence she had found in a suitcase, which could convince Mr. Poe that their Uncle Monty had been murdered. And she was smiling this way now, as she looked up at the strange device on the ceiling, and then back down at the two switches on the wall.

"Watch this," she said, and flicked the first switch. Immediately, the gears began to spin, and the long strip of rubber began to move, and the wheel of mirrors became a whirring circle.

"But what does it do?" Klaus said.

"Listen," Violet said, and the children could hear a low, buzzing hum coming from the machine. "That's the hum Count Olaf was talking about. He thought it was coming from the crystal ball, but it was coming from this invention."

"I thought a magical hum sounded fishy," Klaus said.

"Legror?" Sunny asked, which meant "But what about the lightning?"

"You see how that larger mirror is angled?" Violet said. "It's pointed so that it reflects any light that comes out of the small hole in the tent."

"But there isn't any light coming from it," Klaus said.

"Not now," Violet said, "because the hole is facing east, and it's late in the afternoon. But in the morning, when Madame Lulu does her fortune-telling, the sun is rising, and the light of the sunrise would shine right on that mirror. And that mirror would reflect it onto the other mirrors, put into motion by the torquated belt—"

"Wait," Klaus said. "I don't understand."

"That's O.K.," Violet said. "Count Olaf doesn't understand either. When he walks into the tent in the morning, Madame Lulu turns this invention on and the room is filled with flickering lights. Remember when I used the refraction of light to make a signaling device at Lake Lachrymose? It's the same thing, but Lulu tells him that it's magical lightning."

"But wouldn't Olaf look up and see that it wasn't magical lightning?"

"Not if the lights were off," Violet said, flicking the other switch, and above them the stars went out. The cloth of the tent was so thick that no light from outside shone in, and the Baudelaires found themselves in utter darkness. It reminded the children of when they were climbing down the elevator shaft of 667 Dark Avenue, except that had been silent, and here they were surrounded by the sound of the machine's hum.

"Eerie," Sunny said.

"It *is* spooky," Klaus agreed. "No wonder Olaf thought it was a magical hum."

"Imagine how it would feel if the room were flickering with lightning," Violet said. "That's the sort of trickery that makes people believe in fortune-telling."

"So Madame Lulu is a fake," Klaus said.

Violet flicked both switches again, and the lights went on as the invention went off. "She's a fake, all right," Violet said. "I bet that crystal ball is just plain glass. She tricks Count Olaf into thinking she's a fortune-teller, so he'll buy her things like lions and new turbans."

"Chesro?" Sunny asked, and looked up at her siblings. By "Chesro?" Sunny meant something along the lines of, "But if she's a fake, how did she know that one of our parents was alive?" but her siblings were almost afraid to answer her.

"She didn't, Sunny," Violet said quietly. "Madame Lulu's information is as fake as her magic lightning."

Sunny made a small, quiet sound that her siblings could scarcely hear behind her beard, and hugged Violet and Klaus's legs while her little body shivered with sadness. Suddenly, it was Sunny's turn to bear the burden of Baudelaire grief, but she did not bear it for long, because Klaus thought of something that made the Baudelaires collect themselves.

"Wait a minute," Klaus said. "Madame Lulu may be a fake, but her information might be real. After all, she always told Count Olaf where we were staying, and she was right about that."

"That's true," Violet said. "I forgot about that."

"After all," Klaus said, reaching with difficulty into his pocket. "We first thought that one of our parents might be alive after we read this." He unfolded a piece of paper that his sisters recognized as the thirteenth page of the Snicket file. There was a photograph, stapled to the page, which showed the Baudelaire parents, standing next to one man the Baudelaires had met briefly at the Village of Fowl Devotees, and one man the children did not recognize, and below the photograph was a sentence Klaus had read so many times that he did not need his glasses to read it again. "'Because of the evidence discussed on page nine, experts now suspect that there may in fact be one survivor of the fire, but the survivor's whereabouts are unknown,'" he recited. "Maybe Madame Lulu knows about this."

"But how?" Violet asked.

"Well, let's see," Klaus said. "Count Olaf said that after the appearance of magical lightning, Madame Lulu told him to close his eyes so she could concentrate."

"There!" Sunny said, pointing to the table with the crystal ball.

"No, Sunny," Violet said. "The crystal ball couldn't tell her. It's not magical, remember?"

"There!" Sunny insisted, and walked over to the table. Violet and Klaus followed her, walking awkwardly, and saw what she was pointing at. Sticking out from under the table-cloth was a tiny speck of white. Kneeling down in their shared pants, the older Baudelaires could see it was the very edge of a piece of paper.

"Good thing you're closer to the ground than we are, Sunny," said Klaus. "We never would have noticed that."

"But what is it?" Violet asked, sliding it out from under the tablecloth.

Klaus reached into his pocket again, re-moved his glasses, and put them on. "Now I feel less like a freak and more like myself," he said with a smile, and began to read out loud. "'My Dear Duchess, Your masked ball sounds like a fantastic evening, and I look forward to . . .'" His voice trailed off, and he scanned the rest of the page. "It's just a note about some party," he said.

"What's it doing underneath a tablecloth?" Violet asked.

"It doesn't seem important to me," Klaus

said, "but I guess it was important enough to Lulu that she hid it.

"Let's see what else she's hiding," Violet said, and lifted the end of the tablecloth. All three Baudelaires gasped.

It may seem strange to read that there was a library underneath Madame Lulu's table, but as the Baudelaire orphans knew, there are almost as many kinds of libraries as there are kinds of readers. The children had encountered a private library at the home of Justice Strauss, who they missed very much, and a scientific library at the home of Uncle Monty, who they would never see again. They had seen an academic library at Prufrock Preparatory School, and a library at Lucky Smells Lumbermill that was understocked, a word which here means "empty except for three books." There are public libraries and medical libraries, secret libraries and forbidden libraries, libraries of records and libraries of auction catalogs, and there are archival libraries, which is a fancy term for a collection of files and documents rather than books. Archival libraries are usually found at universities, museums, or other quiet places—such as underneath a table—where people can go and examine whatever papers they like, in order to find the information they need. The Baudelaire orphans gazed at the enormous piles of papers that were stuffed underneath the table, and realized that Madame Lulu had an archival library that just might contain the information they were looking for.

"Look at all this," Violet said. "There are newspaper articles, magazines, letters, files, photographs—all sorts of documents. Madame Lulu tells people to close their eyes and concentrate, and then she looks through all this material and finds the answers."

"And they can't hear her shuffling paper," Klaus said, "over the hum of the lightning device."

"It's like taking a test," Violet said, "with all

the answers hidden in your school desk."

"Cheat!" Sunny said.

"It *is* cheating," Klaus said, "but maybe her cheating can help us. Look, here's an article from *The Daily Punctilio*."

"VILLAGE OF FOWL DEVOTEES TO PARTICI-PATE IN NEW GUARDIAN PROGRAM," Violet said, peering over his shoulder at the headline.

"'The Council of Elders announced yesterday that they would care for the troublesome Baudelaire orphans,'" Klaus read, "'as part of the city government's new program inspired by the aphorism "It takes a village to raise a child."'"

"That's how Count Olaf found us!" Violet said. "Madame Lulu pretended that the crystal ball told her where we were, but she just read it in the newspaper!"

Klaus flipped through a pile of paper until he saw his own name on a list. "Look," he said. "It's a list of new students at Prufrock Preparatory School. Somehow Madame Lulu got ahold of it and passed on the information to Olaf."

"Us!" Sunny said, showing a photograph to her siblings. Violet and Klaus looked at it and saw their sister was right. The youngest Baudelaire had found a small, blurry photograph of the three Baudelaires sitting on the edge of Damocles Dock, where they had arrived for their stay with Aunt Josephine. In the background they could see Mr. Poe reaching his hand out to call for a taxi, while Violet stared glumly into a paper sack.

"Those are the peppermints Mr. Poe gave us," Violet said quietly. "I'd almost forgotten about those."

"But who took this?" Klaus asked. "Who was watching us that day?"

"Back," Sunny said, and turned the photograph over. On the back, someone had written something in messy handwriting the children could scarcely read.

"I think it says, 'This might be hopeful,'" Klaus said.

"Or 'helpful,'" Violet said. "'This might be helpful.' And it's signed with one initial—I think it's an R, or maybe a K. But who would want a photograph of us?"

"It gives me the shivers to think someone took our picture when we didn't know it," Klaus said. "That means someone could be taking our photograph at any moment."

The Baudelaires looked around hurriedly, but could see no photographer lurking in the tent. "Let's calm down," Violet said. "Remember the time we watched a scary movie when our parents were out for the evening, and we were jumpy for the rest of the night? Every time we heard a noise we thought vampires were breaking into the house to take us away."

"Maybe somebody *was* breaking into the house to take us away," Klaus said, and pointed to the photograph. "Sometimes things can go on right in front of your nose, but you don't know about them."

"Heebie-jeebies," Sunny said, which meant

something like, "Let's get out of here. I'm really getting the creeps."

"Me, too," Violet said, "but let's take all these documents with us. Maybe we can find someplace to look through them and find the information we want."

"We can't take all these papers with us," Klaus said. "There are stacks and stacks. It would be like checking out every single book in the library, just to find the one you wanted to read."

"We'll stuff our pockets," Violet said.

"My pockets are already stuffed," Klaus said. "I have page thirteen of the Snicket file, and all those fragments from the Quagmire notebooks. I can't get rid of those, but I don't have room for anything else. It's as if all the world's secrets are here on paper, but which secrets do we take with us?"

"Maybe we can look through it quickly right here," Violet said, "and take anything that has our names on it."

"That's not the best method of research," Klaus said, "but I guess it will have to do. Here, help me lift the tablecloth so we can see everything better."

Violet and Klaus began to lift the tablecloth together, but it was quite difficult to do in their disguise. Like eating an ear of corn, lifting the tablecloth while sharing a shirt was trickier than it looked, and the tablecloth slid back and forth as the older Baudelaires struggled with it. As I'm sure you know, if you slide a tablecloth back and forth, the things sitting on the tablecloth will slide, too, and Madame Lulu's crystal ball began to slide closer and closer to the edge of the table.

"Mishap," Sunny said.

"Sunny's right," Violet said. "Let's be careful."

"Right," Klaus said. "We don't want—"

Klaus did not get to finish his sentence about what he and his sisters did not want, because with a dull *thunk* and a loud, clattering *crash!* his sentence was finished for him. One of the most troublesome things in life is that what you do or do not want has very little to do with what does or does not happen. You might want to become the sort of author who works calmly at home, for example, but something could happen that would lead you to become the sort of author who works frantically in the homes of other people, often without their knowledge. You might want to marry someone you love very much, but something could happen that would prevent the two of you from ever seeing one another again. You might want to find out something important about your parents, but something could happen that would mean you wouldn't find out for quite some time. And you might want, at a particular moment, for a crystal ball not to fall off a table and shatter into a thousand pieces, and even if it happened that the crystal ball did shatter, you might want the sound not to attract anyone's attention. But the sad truth is that the truth is sad, and that what you want does not matter. A series of unfortunate events can happen to anyone, no matter what they want, and even though the three children did not want the flap of the fortune-telling tent to open, and they did not want Madame Lulu to step inside, as the afternoon turned to evening at Caligari Carnival, everything happened to the Baudelaire orphans that they did not want at all.

CHAPTER Seven

"*What* are you doing here, please?" Madame Lulu snarled. She strode quickly toward them, her own eyes glaring as angrily as the eye she was wearing around her neck. "What are the freaks doing in the tent, please, and what are the freaks doing under the table, please, and please answer me this instant, please, or you will be very, very sorry, please, thank you!"

The Baudelaire orphans looked up at the fake fortune-teller, and a strange thing happened. Rather than quaking with fear, or crying

out in horror, or huddling together as Lulu shrieked at them, the three children stood resolute, a phrase which here means "did not become frightened at all." Now that they knew that Madame Lulu used a machine on her ceiling and an archival library under her table to disguise herself as a magical and mysterious person, it was as if every frightening thing about her had melted away, and she was just a woman with an odd accent and a bad temper who had crucial information the Baudelaires needed. As Madame Lulu carried on, Violet, Klaus, and Sunny watched her without a terrified thought in their heads. Madame Lulu yelled and yelled, but the children felt just as angry at Lulu as Lulu was at them.

"How dare you, please, enter the tent without permission of Madame Lulu!" Madame Lulu cried. "I am the boss of Caligari Carnival, please, and you must obey me every single moment of your freakish lives! Please, I have never seen, please, the freaks who are so ungrateful to Madame Lulu! You are in the worst of the trouble, please!" By now, Lulu had reached the table, and saw the pile of broken glass which sparkled all over the floor. "You are the breakers of the crystal ball!" she bellowed, pointing a dirty fingernail at the Baudelaires. "You should be ashamed of your freaky selves! The crystal ball is the very valuable thing, please, and is having of the magical powers!"

"Fraud!" Sunny cried.

"That crystal ball wasn't magical!" Violet translated angrily. "It was plain glass! And you're not a real fortune-teller, either! We analyzed your lightning device, and we found your archival library."

"This is all one big disguise," Klaus said, gesturing around the tent. "*You're* the one who should be ashamed of yourself."

"Ple—" Madame Lulu said, but she shut her mouth before she could finish the word. She looked down at the Baudelaires, and her eyes grew very wide. Then she sat down in a chair, lay her head down next to the crystal ball, and began to cry. "I am ashamed of myself," she said, in an unaccented voice, and reached up to her turban. With a flick of her wrist, she unraveled the turban, and her long, blond hair fell down around her tearstained face. "I am utterly ashamed of myself," she said, through her tears, and her shoulders shook with sobs.

The Baudelaires looked at one another and then at the quaking woman sitting near them. It is hard for decent people to stay angry at someone who has burst into tears, which is why it is often a good idea to burst into tears if a decent person is yelling at you. The three children watched as Madame Lulu cried and cried, pausing only to wipe her eyes with her sleeves, and they could not help but feel a little bit sad, too, even as their anger continued.

"Madame Lulu," Violet said firmly, although not as firmly as she would have liked, "why did you—"

"Oh," Madame Lulu cried, at the sound of

her name, "don't call me that." She reached up to her neck and yanked on the cord that held the eye around her neck. It broke with a *snap!* and she dropped it to the ground where it lay amid the pieces of shattered glass while she went on sobbing. "My name is Olivia," she said finally, with a shuddering sigh. "I'm not Madame Lulu and I'm not a fortune-teller."

"But why are you pretending to be these things?" Klaus asked. "Why are you wearing a disguise? Why are you helping Count Olaf?"

"I try to help everyone," Olivia said sadly. "My motto is 'give people what they want.' That's why I'm here at the carnival. I pretend to be a fortune-teller, and tell people whatever it is they want to hear. If Count Olaf or one of his henchmen steps inside and asks me where the Baudelaires are, I tell them. If Jacques Snicket or another volunteer steps inside and asks me if his brother is alive, I tell them."

The Baudelaires felt so many questions tripping up inside them that they could scarcely decide which one to ask. "But where do you learn the answers?" Violet asked, pointing to the piles of paper underneath the table. "Where does all this information come from?"

"Libraries, mostly," Olivia said, wiping her eyes. "If you want people to think you're a fortune-teller, you have to answer their questions, and the answer to nearly every question is written down someplace. It just might take a while to find. It's taken me a long time to gather my archival library, and I still don't have all of the answers I've been looking for. So sometimes, when someone asks me a question and I don't know the answer, I just make something up."

"When you told Count Olaf that one of our parents was alive," Klaus asked, "were you making it up, or did you know the answer?"

Olivia frowned. "Count Olaf didn't ask anything about the parents of any carnival frea— wait a minute. Your voices sound different. Beverly, you have a ribbon in your hair, and your other head is wearing glasses. What's going on?"

The three children looked at one another in surprise. They had been so interested in what Olivia was saying that they had completely forgotten about their disguises, but now it appeared that disguises might not be necessary. The siblings needed to have their questions answered honestly, and it seemed more likely that Olivia would give them honest answers if the children were honest themselves. Without speaking, the Baudelaires stood up and removed their disguises. Violet and Klaus unbuttoned the shirt they were sharing, stretching the arms they had been keeping cooped up, and then stepped out of the fur-cuffed pants, while Sunny unwrapped the beard from around her. In no time at all the Baudelaires were standing in the tent in their regular clothing—except for Violet, who was still wearing a hospital gown from her stay in the Surgical Ward—with their disguises on the floor in a heap. The older Baudelaires even shook their heads vigorously, a word which here means "in order to shake talcum powder out of their hair," and rubbed at their faces so their disguised scars would disappear.

"I'm not really Beverly," Violet said, "and this is my brother, not my other head. And that's not Chabo the Wolf Baby. She's—"

"I know who she is," Olivia said, looking at all of them amazedly. "I know who all of you are. You're the Baudelaires!"

"Yes," Klaus said, and he and his sisters smiled. It felt as if it had been one hundred years since someone had called the Baudelaires by their proper names, and when Olivia recognized them, it was as if they were finally themselves again, instead of carnival freaks or any other fake identity. "Yes," Klaus said again. "We're the Baudelaires—three of them, anyway. We're not sure, but we think there may be a fourth. We think one of our parents may be alive."

"Not sure?" Olivia asked. "Isn't the answer in the Snicket file?"

"We just have the last page of the Snicket

file," Klaus said, and pulled page thirteen out of his pocket again. "We're trying to find the rest of it before Olaf does. But the last page says that there may be a survivor of the fire. Do you know if that's true?"

"I have no idea," Olivia admitted. "I've been looking for the Snicket file myself. Every time I see a piece of paper blow by, I chase after it to see if it's one of the pages."

"But you told Count Olaf that one of our parents is alive," Violet said, "and that they're hiding in the Mortmain Mountains."

"I was just guessing," Olivia said. "If one of your parents has survived, though, that's probably where they'd be. Somewhere in the Mortmain Mountains is one of the last surviving headquarters of V.F.D. But you know that, of course."

"We don't know that," Klaus said. "We don't even know what V.F.D. stands for."

"Then how did you learn to disguise yourselves?" Olivia asked in astonishment. "You used

all three phases of V.F.D. Disguise Training—
veiled facial disguises, with your fake scars, various finery disguises, with the clothing you
wore, and voice fakery disguises, with the different voices you used. Now that I think of it,
you're even using disguises that look like things
in my disguise kit."

Olivia stood up and walked over to the
trunk that sat in the corner. Taking a key out of
her pocket, she unlocked it and began to go
through its contents. The siblings watched as
she lifted an assortment of things out of the
trunk, all of which the children recognized.
First she removed a wig that looked like the
one Count Olaf had used when he was pretending to be a woman named Shirley, and then
a fake wooden leg he had used as part of his
ship captain disguise. She removed a pair of
pots that Olaf's bald associate had used when
the children were living in Paltryville, and a
motorcycle helmet that looked identical to the
one Esmé Squalor had used to disguise herself

as a police officer. Finally, Olivia held up a shirt with fancy ruffles all over it, exactly like the one that lay at the Baudelaires' feet. "You see," she said. "This is the same shirt as the one you two were wearing."

"But we got ours from Count Olaf's trunk," Violet said.

"That makes sense," Olivia replied. "All volunteers have the same disguise kit. There are people using these disguises all over the world, trying to bring Count Olaf to justice."

"What?" Sunny asked.

"I'm confused, too," Klaus said. "We're all confused, Olivia. What is V.F.D.? Sometimes it seems like they're good people, and sometimes it seems like they're bad people."

"It's not as simple as all that," Olivia said sadly. She took a surgical mask out of the trunk and held it in her hand. "The items in the disguise kit are just things, Baudelaires. You can use these things to help people or to harm them, and many people use them to do both. Sometimes it's hard to know which disguise to use, or what to do once you've put one on."

"I don't understand," Violet said.

"Some people are like those lions Olaf brought here," Olivia said. "They start out being good people, but before they know it they've become something else. Those lions used to be noble creatures. A friend of mine trained them to smell smoke, which was very helpful in our work. But now Count Olaf is denying them food, and hitting them with his whip, and tomorrow afternoon they'll probably devour one of the freaks. The world is a harum-scarum place."

"Harum?" Sunny asked.

"It's complicated and confusing," Olivia explained. "They say that long ago it was simple and quiet, but that might be a legend. There was a schism in V.F.D.—a great big fight between many of the members—and since then it's been hard for me to know what to do. I never thought I'd be the sort of person who helps villains, but now I do. Haven't you ever found yourself doing something you never thought you'd do?"

"I guess so," Klaus said, and turned to his sisters. "Remember when we stole those keys from Hal, at the Library of Records? I never thought I'd be a thief."

"Flynn," Sunny said, which meant something like, "And I never thought I would become a violent person, but I engaged in a sword fight with Dr. Orwell."

"We've all done things we never thought we'd do," Violet said, "but we always had a good reason."

"Everybody thinks they have a good reason," Olivia said. "Count Olaf thinks getting a fortune is a good reason to slaughter you. Esmé Squalor thinks being Olaf's girlfriend is a good reason to join his troupe. And when I told Count Olaf where to find you, I had a good reason—because my motto is 'give people what they want.'"

"Dubious," Sunny said.

"Sunny's not sure that's a very good reason," Violet translated, "and I must say I agree with her. You've caused a lot of grief, Olivia, to a lot of people, just so you could give Count Olaf what he wanted."

Olivia nodded, and tears appeared in her eyes once more. "I know it," she said miserably. "I'm ashamed of myself. But I don't know what else to do."

"You could stop helping Olaf," Klaus said, "and help us instead. You could tell us everything you know about V.F.D. And you could take us to the Mortmain Mountains to see if one of our parents is really alive."

"I don't know," Olivia said. "I've behaved so badly for so long, but maybe I could change." She stood up straight, and looked sadly around the darkening tent. "I used to be a noble person," she said. "Do you think I could be noble again?"

"I don't know," Klaus said, "but let's find

out. We could leave together, right now, and head north."

"But how?" Olivia asked. "We don't have a car, or a minivan, or four horses, or a large sling-shot, or any other way to get out of the hinter-lands."

Violet retied the ribbon in her hair, and looked up at the ceiling in thought. "Olivia," she said finally, "do the carts on that roller coaster still work?"

"The carts?" Olivia repeated. "Sort of. The wheels move, but there's a small engine in each cart, and I think the engines have rusted away."

"I think I could rebuild an engine using your lightning device," Violet said. "After all, that piece of rubber is a bit like—"

"A fan belt!" Olivia finished. "That's a good idea, Violet."

"I'll sneak out to the roller coaster tonight," Violet said, "and get to work. We'll leave in the morning, before anyone gets up."

"Better not do it tonight," Olivia said.

"Count Olaf or his henchmen are always lurking around at night. It'd be better to leave in the afternoon, when everyone is at the House of Freaks. You can put the invention together first thing in the morning, when Olaf will be in here asking the crystal ball about you."

"What will you do then?" Klaus asked.

"I have a spare crystal ball," Olivia answered. "That isn't the first one that's been broken."

"That's not what I mean," Klaus said. "I mean, you won't tell Count Olaf that we're here at the carnival, will you?"

Olivia paused for a moment, and shook her head. "No," she said, but she did not sound very sure.

"Promise?" Sunny asked.

Olivia looked down at the youngest Baudelaire for a long time without answering. "Yes," she finally said, in a very quiet voice. "I promise, if you promise to take me with you to find V.F.D."

"We promise," Violet said, and her siblings

nodded in agreement. "Now, let's start at the beginning. What does V.F.D. stand for?"

"Madame Lulu!" called a scratchy voice from outside the tent. The Baudelaires looked at one another in dismay as Count Olaf called the fake name of the woman beside them. "Madame Lulu! Where are you?"

"I am in fortune-telling tent, my Olaf," Olivia replied, slipping into her accent as easily as the Baudelaires could slip into the ruffled shirt. "But do not come in, please. I am doing secret ritual with crystal ball of mine."

"Well, hurry up," Olaf said grumpily. "The pit is done, and I'm very thirsty. Come pour us all some wine."

"Just one minute, my Olaf," Olivia said, reaching down to grab the material for her turban. "Why don't you be taking of a shower, please? You must be sweaty from the pit digging, and when you are done we will all be having of the wine together."

"Don't be ridiculous," Count Olaf replied.

"I took a shower ten days ago. I'll go put on some extra cologne and meet you in your caravan."

"Yes, my Olaf," Olivia called, and then turned to whisper to the children as she wound the turban around her hair. "We'd better cut short our conversation," she said. "The others will be looking for you. When we leave here tomorrow, I'll tell you everything you want to know."

"Couldn't you just tell us a few things now?" Klaus asked. The Baudelaires had never been closer to the answers they were seeking, and delaying things any further was almost more than they could stand.

"No, no," Olivia decided. "Here, I'd better help you get back into your disguises or you'll get caught."

The three children looked at one another reluctantly. "I guess you're right," Violet said finally. "The others will be looking for us."

"Proffco," Sunny said, which meant "I guess

so," and began to wind the beard around her. Violet and Klaus stepped into the fur-cuffed pants, and buttoned the shirt around them, while Olivia tied her necklace back together so she could become Madame Lulu once more.

"Our scars," Klaus remembered, looking at his sister's face. "We rubbed them off."

"And our hair needs repowdering," Violet said.

"I have a makeup pencil, please," Olivia said, reaching into the trunk, "and also the powder of talcum."

"You don't have to use your accent right now," Violet said, taking the ribbon out of her hair.

"Is good to practice, please," Olivia replied. "I must be thinking of myself as Madame Lulu, otherwise I will please be forgetting of the disguise."

"But you'll remember our promises, won't you?" Klaus asked.

"Promises?" Madame Lulu repeated.

"You promised you wouldn't tell Count Olaf that we're here," Violet said, "and we promised to take you with us to the Mortmain Mountains."

"Of course, Beverly," Madame Lulu replied. "I will be keeping of the promise to freaks."

"I'm not Beverly," Violet said, "and I'm not a freak."

Madame Lulu smiled, and leaned in to pencil a scar on the eldest Baudelaire's face. "But it is time for disguises, please," she said. "Don't be forgetting of your disguised voices, or you will be recognized."

"We won't forget our disguises," Klaus said, putting his glasses back in his pocket, "and you won't forget your promise, right?"

"Of course, please," Madame Lulu said, leading the children out of the fortune-telling tent. "Do not be of the worrying, please."

The siblings stepped out of the tent with Madame Lulu, and found themselves bathed in the blue light of the famous hinterlands sunset.

The light made each of them look a bit different, as if they were wearing another blue disguise on top of their carnival disguises. The powder in Violet's hair made her head look a pale, strange color, Klaus's fake scars looked darker and more sinister in the shadows, and Sunny looked like a small blue cloud, with small sparks of light where her teeth reflected the last of the sun. And Madame Lulu looked more like a fortune-teller, as the sunset glistened on the jewel in her turban, and shone on her long robe in an eerie light that looked almost magical.

"Good night, my freaky ones," she said, and the Baudelaires looked at this mysterious woman and wondered if she had really changed her motto, and would become a noble person once more. "I will be keeping of the promise," Madame Lulu said, but the Baudelaire orphans did not know if she was speaking the truth, or just telling them what they wanted to hear.

CHAPTER

Eight

By the time the Baudelaire
orphans found their way back
to the freaks' caravan, Hugo,
Colette, and Kevin were waiting for them. Colette and Kevin
were just finishing a game of
dominoes, and Hugo had cooked
up a pot of tom ka gai, which is a
delicious soup commonly eaten in
Thailand. But as the Baudelaires sat
at the table and ate their supper, they
were not in the mood to digest the
mixture of chicken, vegetables, fancy

mushrooms, fresh ginger, coconut milk, and water chestnuts that the hunchback had pre-pared. They were more concerned with digest-ing information, a phrase which here means "thinking about everything that Madame Lulu had told them." Violet took a spoonful of hot broth, but she was thinking so hard about Lulu's archival library that she scarcely noticed the unusual, sweet taste. Klaus chewed on a water chestnut, but he was wondering so much about the headquarters in the Mortmain Mountains that he didn't appreciate its appealing, crunchy texture. And Sunny tipped the bowl forward to take a large sip, but she was so curious about the disguise kit that she wasn't aware that her beard was getting soaked. Each of the three children finished their soup to the last drop, but they were so eager to hear more from Lulu about the mystery of V.F.D. that they felt hungrier than when they sat down.

"Everyone sure is quiet tonight," Colette said, contorting her head underneath her armpit to look around the table. "Hugo and Kevin, you haven't talked much, and I don't think I've heard a single growl from Chabo, or heard a word out of either of your heads."

"I guess we're not feeling much like making conversation," Violet said, remembering to speak as low as she could. "We have a lot to think about."

"We sure do," Hugo said. "I'm still not wild about the idea of being eaten by a lion."

"Me neither," Colette said, "but today's visitors were certainly excited about the carnival's new attraction. Everyone does seem to love violence."

"And sloppy eating," Hugo said, dabbing at his mouth with a napkin. "It's certainly an interesting dilemma."

"I don't think it's an interesting dilemma," Klaus said, squinting at his coworkers. "I think it's a terrible one. Tomorrow afternoon, someone will jump to their deaths." He did not add that the Baudelaires planned to be far away from

Caligari Carnival by then, heading out to the Mortmain Mountains in the invention Violet planned to construct early tomorrow morning.

"I don't know what we can do about it," Kevin said. "On one hand, I'd rather keep on performing at the House of Freaks instead of being fed to the lions. But on the other hand— and in my case, both my hands are equally strong—Madame Lulu's motto is 'give people what they want,' and apparently they want this carnival to be carnivorous."

"I think it's a terrible motto," Violet said, and Sunny growled in agreement. "There are better things to do with your life than doing something humiliating and dangerous, just to make total strangers happy."

"Like what?" Colette asked.

The Baudelaires looked at one another. They were afraid to reveal their plan to their coworkers, in case one of them would tell Count Olaf and ruin their escape. But they also couldn't stand resolute, knowing that something terrible would happen just because Hugo, Colette, and Kevin felt obliged to be freaks and live up to Madame Lulu's motto.

"You never know when you'll find something else to do," Violet said finally. "It could happen at any moment."

"Do you really think so?" Hugo asked hopefully.

"Yes," Klaus said. "You never know when opportunity will knock."

Kevin looked up from his soup and gazed at the Baudelaires with a look of hope in his eye. "Which hand will it knock with?"

"Opportunity can knock with any hand, Kevin," Klaus said, and at that moment there was a knock at the door.

"Open up, freaks." The impatient voice, coming from outside the caravan, made the children jump. As I'm sure you know, when Klaus used the expression "opportunity will knock," he meant that his coworkers might find something better to do with their time, instead of leaping into a pit of hungry lions just to give some people what they wanted. He did not mean that the girlfriend of a notorious villain would actually knock on the door and give them an idea that was possibly even worse, but I am sorry to say that it was Esmé Squalor who was knocking, her long fingernails clattering against the door. "Open up. I want to talk to you."

"Just one moment, Ms. Squalor," Hugo called, and walked over to the door. "Let's all be on our best behavior," he said to his co-workers. "It's not often that a normal person wants to talk to us, and I think we should make the most of this opportunity."

"We'll be good," Colette promised. "I won't bend into a single strange position."

"And I'll use only my right hand," Kevin said. "Or maybe only my left hand."

"Good idea," Hugo said, and opened the door. Esmé Squalor was leaning in the doorway with a wicked smile on her face.

"I am Esmé Gigi Geniveve Squalor," she

said, which was often how she announced herself, even when everyone nearby knew who she was. She stepped inside the freaks' caravan, and the Baudelaires could see that she had dressed for the occasion, a phrase which here means "put on a specific outfit in an attempt to impress them." She was dressed in a long, white gown, so long that it passed her feet and lay around her as if she were standing in a large puddle of milk. Embroidered on the front of the gown in glittery thread were the words I LOVE FREAKS, except instead of the word "love" there was an enormous heart, a symbol sometimes used by people who have trouble figuring out the difference between words and shapes. On one of the shoulders of the gown, Esmé had tied a large brown sack, and on her head she had an odd round hat, with black thread poking out of the top, and it had a large, angry face drawn on the front of it. The children knew that such an outfit must be very in, otherwise Esmé would not be wearing it, but they couldn't imagine who in the world would admire such strange clothing.

"What a lovely outfit!" Hugo said.

"Thank you," Esmé said. She poked Colette with one of her long fingernails, and the contortionist stood up so Esmé could sit down in her chair. "As you can see from the front of my gown, I love freaks."

"You do?" Kevin said. "That's very nice of you."

"Yes, it is," Esmé agreed. "I had this dress made especially to show how much I love them. Look, there's a cushion on the shoulder, to resemble a hunchback, and my hat makes me look as if I have two heads, like Beverly and Elliot."

"You certainly look very freakish," Colette said.

Esmé frowned, as if this wasn't quite what she wanted to hear. "Of course, I'm not really a freak," she said. "I'm a normal person, but I wanted to show you all how much I admire you. Now, please bring me a carton of buttermilk. It's very in."

"We don't have any," Hugo said, "but I think we have some cranberry juice, or I could make you some hot chocolate. Chabo here taught me to add cinnamon to the hot chocolate, and it tastes quite delicious."

"Tom ka gai!" Sunny said.

"And we also have soup," Hugo said.

Esmé looked down at Sunny and frowned. "No, thank you," she said, "although it's very kind of you to offer. In fact, you freaks are so kind that I consider you to be more than employees at a carnival I happen to be visiting. I consider you to be some of my closest friends."

The children knew, of course, that this ridiculous statement was as fake as Esmé's second head, but their coworkers were thrilled. Hugo gave Esmé a big smile, and stood up straight so that you could barely see his hunchback. Kevin blushed and looked down at his hands. And Colette was so excited that before she could stop herself, she twisted her body

until it resembled the letter K and the letter S
at the same time.

"Oh, Esmé," Colette said. "Do you really
mean it?"

"Of course I mean it," Esmé said, pointing
to the front of her gown. "I would rather be here
with you than with the finest people in the
world."

"Gosh," Kevin said. "No normal person has
ever called me a friend."

"Well, that's what you are," Esmé said, and
leaned toward Kevin to kiss him on the nose.
"You're all my freaky friends. And it makes me
very sad to think that one of you will be eaten
by lions tomorrow." The Baudelaires watched
as she reached into a pocket in the gown and
drew out a white handkerchief, embroidered
with the same slogan as her gown, and held up
the word "freaks" to dab at her eyes. "I have
real tears in my eyes from thinking about it,"
she explained.

"There, there, close friend," Kevin said, and

patted one of her hands. "Don't be sad."

"I can't help it," Esmé said, yanking back her own hand as if she were afraid that being ambidextrous was contagious. "But I have an opportunity for you that might make all of us very, very happy."

"An opportunity?" Hugo asked. "Why, Beverly and Elliot were just telling us that an opportunity could come along at any minute."

"And they were right," Esmé said. "Tonight I am offering you the opportunity to quit your jobs at the House of Freaks, and join Count Olaf and myself in his troupe."

"What would we do exactly?" Hugo asked.

Esmé smiled, and began to accentuate the positive aspects of working with Count Olaf, a phrase which here means "make the opportunity sound better than it really was, by emphasizing the good parts and scarcely mentioning the bad." "It's a theatrical troupe," she said, "so you'd be wearing costumes and doing dramatic exercises, and occasionally committing crimes."

"Dramatic exercises!" Kevin exclaimed, clasping both hands to his heart. "It's always been my heart's desire to perform on a stage!"

"And I've always wanted to wear a costume!" Hugo said.

"But you do perform on a stage," Violet said, "and you wear an ill-fitting costume every day at the House of Freaks."

"If you joined, you'd get to travel with us to exciting places," Esmé continued, glaring at Violet. "Members of Count Olaf's troupe have seen the trees of Finite Forest, and the shores of Lake Lachrymose, and the crows of the Village of Fowl Devotees, although they always have to sit in the back seat. And, best of all, you'd get to work for Count Olaf, one of the most brilliant and handsome men who ever walked the face of the earth."

"Do you really think that a normal man like him would want to work with freaks like us?" Colette asked.

"Of course he would," Esmé said. "Count

Olaf doesn't care whether you have something wrong with you or if you're normal, as long as you're willing to carry out his orders. I think you'll find that working in Olaf's troupe is a job where people won't think you're freakish at all. And you'll be paid a fortune—at least, Count Olaf will be."

"Wow!" Hugo said. "What an opportunity!"

"I had a hunch you'd be excited about it," Esmé said. "No offense, Hugo. Now, if you're interested in joining, there's just one thing you need to do."

"A job interview?" Colette asked nervously.

"There's no need for close friends of mine to do anything as unpleasant as a job interview," Esmé said. "You just have to do one simple task. Tomorrow afternoon, during the show with the lions, Count Olaf will announce which freak will jump into the pit of lions. But I want whomever is chosen to throw Madame Lulu in instead."

The freaks' caravan was silent for a moment as everyone digested this information. "You mean," Hugo said finally, "that you want us to murder Madame Lulu?"

"Don't think of it as murder," Esmé said. "Think of it as a dramatic exercise. It's a special surprise for Count Olaf that will prove to him that you're brave enough to join his troupe."

"Throwing Lulu into a pit of lions doesn't strike me as particularly brave," Colette said. "Just cruel and vicious."

"How can it be cruel and vicious to give people what they want?" Esmé asked. "You want to join Count Olaf's troupe, the crowd wants to see someone eaten by lions, and I want Madame Lulu thrown into the pit. Tomorrow, one of you will have the exciting opportunity to give everybody exactly what they want."

"Grr," Sunny growled, but only her siblings understood that she really meant "Everybody except Lulu."

"When you put it like that," Hugo said thoughtfully, "it doesn't sound so bad."

"Of course it doesn't," Esmé said, adjusting

her false head. "Besides, Madame Lulu was eager to see all of you eaten by lions, so you should be happy to throw her in the pit."

"But why do you want Madame Lulu thrown in?" Colette asked.

Esmé scowled. "Count Olaf thinks we have to make this carnival popular, so that Madame Lulu will help us with her crystal ball," she said, "but I don't think we need her help. Besides, I'm tired of my boyfriend buying her presents."

"That doesn't seem like such a good reason for someone to be eaten by lions," Violet said carefully, in her disguised voice.

"I'm not surprised that a two-headed person like yourself is a little confused," Esmé said, and reached out her long-nailed hands to pat both Violet and Klaus on their scarred faces. "Once you join Olaf's troupe, you won't be troubled by that kind of freakish thinking any longer."

"Just think," Hugo said, "tomorrow we'll stop being freaks, and we'll be henchmen of Count Olaf."

"I prefer the term henchpeople," Colette said.

Esmé gave everyone in the room a big smile, and then reached up to her shoulder and opened the brown sack. "To celebrate your new jobs," she said, "I brought each of you a present."

"A present!" Kevin cried. "Madame Lulu never gave us presents."

"This is for you, Hugo," Esmé said, and took out an oversized coat the Baudelaires recognized from a time when the hook-handed man had disguised himself as a doorman. The coat was so big that it had covered his hooks, and as Hugo tried it on, they saw that it was also big enough to fit Hugo, even with his irregular shape. Hugo looked at himself in the mirror and then at his coworkers in joy.

"It covers my hunchback!" he said happily. "I look normal, instead of freakish!"

"You see?" Esmé said. "Count Olaf is already making your life much better. And look what I have for you, Colette." The Baudelaires watched as Olaf's girlfriend reached into the sack and pulled out the long, black robe that they had seen in the trunk of the automobile. "It's so baggy," Esmé explained, "that you can twist your body any which way, and no one will notice that you're a contortionist."

"It's like a dream come true!" Colette said, grabbing it out of Esmé's hands. "I'd throw a hundred people into the lion pit to wear something like this."

"And Kevin," Esmé said, "look at this small piece of rope. Turn around, and I'll tie your right hand behind your back so you can't possibly use it."

"And then I'll be left-handed, like normal people!" Kevin said, jumping out of his chair and standing on his two equally strong feet. "Hooray!"

The ambidextrous person turned around happily so Esmé could tie his right hand behind his back, and in a moment he became someone with only one useful arm instead of two.

"I haven't forgotten you two," Esmé continued, smiling at the three of them. "Chabo,
here's a long razor that Count Olaf uses when
he needs to disguise himself with a good shave.
I thought you could use it to trim some of that
ugly wolf hair. And for you, Beverly and Elliot,
I have this."

Esmé removed the sack from her gown
and held it out to the older Baudelaires tri-
umphantly. Violet and Klaus peeked inside and
saw that it was empty. "This sack is perfect to
cover up one of your heads," she explained.
"You'll look like a normal one-headed person
who just happens to have a sack balanced on
their shoulder. Isn't that smashing?"

"I guess so," Klaus said, in his fake high
voice.

"What's the matter with you?" Hugo demanded. "You've been offered an exciting job
and given a generous present, and yet both your
heads are moping around."

"You, too, Chabo," Colette said. "I can see

through your fur that you don't look very enthu-siastic."

"I think this might be an opportunity that we should refuse," Violet said, and her siblings nodded in agreement.

"*What?*" Esmé said sharply.

"It's nothing personal," Klaus added quickly, although not wanting to work for Count Olaf was about as personal as things could get. "It does seem very exciting to work in a theatrical troupe, and Count Olaf does seem like a terrific person."

"Then what's the problem?" Kevin asked.

"Well," Violet said, "I don't think I'm com-fortable throwing Madame Lulu to the lions."

"As her other head, I agree," Klaus said, "and Chabo agrees, too."

"I bet she only half agrees," Hugo said. "I bet her wolf half can't wait to watch her get eaten."

Sunny shook her head and growled as gently as she could, and Violet lifted her up and placed her on the table. "It just doesn't seem right," Violet said. "Madame Lulu isn't the nicest person I know, but I'm not sure she deserves to be devoured."

Esmé gave the older Baudelaires a large, false smile, and leaned forward to pat them each on the head again. "Don't worry your heads over whether or not she deserves to be devoured," she said, and then smiled down at Chabo. "You don't deserve to be half wolf, do you?" she asked. "People don't always get what they deserve in this world."

"It still seems like a wicked thing to do," Klaus said.

"I don't think so," Hugo said. "It's giving people what they want, just like Lulu says."

"Why don't you sleep on it?" Esmé suggested, and stood up from the table. "Right after tomorrow's show, Count Olaf is heading north to the Mortmain Mountains to take care of something important, and if Madame Lulu is eaten by then, you'll be allowed to join him. You can decide in the morning whether you want to be brave members of a theater troupe, or cowardly freaks in a rundown carnival."

"I don't need to sleep on it," Kevin said.

"Me neither," Colette said. "I can decide right now."

"Yes," Hugo agreed. "I want to join Count Olaf."

"I'm glad to hear that," Esmé said. "Maybe you can convince your coworkers to join you in joining me joining him." She looked scornfully at the three children as she opened the door to the caravan. The hinterlands sunset was long over, and there was not a trace of blue light falling on the carnival. "Think about this, Beverly and Elliot, and Chabo, too," she said. "It just might be a wicked thing, throwing Madame Lulu into a pit full of carnivorous lions." Esmé took a step outside, and it was so dark that Olaf's girlfriend looked like a ghost in a long, white gown and a fake extra head. "But if you don't join us, where can you possibly go?"

she asked. The Baudelaire orphans had no answer for Esmé Squalor's terrible question, but Esmé answered it herself, with a long, wicked laugh. "If you don't choose the wicked thing, what in the world will you do?" she asked, and disappeared into the night.

CHAPTER Nine

The curious thing about being told to sleep on it—a phrase which here means, as I'm sure you know, "to go to bed thinking about something and reach a conclusion in the morning"—is that you usually can't. If you are thinking over a dilemma, you are likely to toss and turn all night long, thinking over terrible things that can happen and trying to imagine what in the world you can do about it, and these circumstances are unlikely to result in any sleeping at all. Just last night, I was troubled by a decision involving an eyedropper, a greedy night watchman, and a tray of individual custards, and this morning I am so tired that I can scarcely type these worfs.

And so it was with the Baudelaire orphans that night, after Esmé Squalor had told them to sleep on it, and decide the next morning whether or not to throw Madame Lulu to the lions and join Count Olaf's troupe. The children, of course, had no intention of becoming part of a band of villains, or tossing anyone into a deadly pit. But Esmé had also asked them what in the world they would do if they decided not to join Olaf, and this was the question that kept them tossing and turning in their hammocks, which are particularly uncomfortable places to toss and turn. The Baudelaires hoped that instead of joining Count Olaf, they would travel through the hinterlands in a motorized roller-coaster cart of Violet's invention, accompanied by Madame Lulu, in her undisguised identity of Olivia, along with the archival library from underneath the table of the fortune-telling

tent, in the hopes of finding one of the Baudelaire parents alive and well at the V.F.D. headquarters in the Mortmain Mountains. But this
plan seemed so complicated that the children
worried over all that could go wrong and spoil
the whole thing. Violet thought about the lightning device that she planned to turn into a fan
belt, and worried that there wouldn't be suffi-
cient torque to make the carts move the way
they needed to. Klaus worried that the archival
library wouldn't contain specific directions to
the headquarters, and they would get lost in the
mountains, which were rumored to be enormous, confusing, and filled with wild animals.
Sunny worried that they might not find enough
to eat in the hinterlands. And all three Baudelaires worried that Madame Lulu would not
keep her promise, and would reveal the
orphans' disguise when Count Olaf asked about
them the next morning. The siblings worried
about these things all night, and although in my
case the dessert chef managed to find my hotel

room and knock on my window just before
dawn, the Baudelaire orphans found that when
morning came and they were done sleeping on
it, they hadn't reached any other conclusion but
that their plan was risky, and the only one they
could think of.

As the first rays of the sun shone through
the window onto the potted plants, the Baudelaires quietly lowered themselves out of their
hammocks. Hugo, Colette, and Kevin had announced that they were ready to join Count
Olaf's troupe and didn't need to sleep on it, and
as so often happens with people who have nothing to sleep on, the children's coworkers were
sleeping soundly and did not awaken as the siblings left the caravan to get to work on their
plan.

Count Olaf and his troupe had dug the lions'
pit alongside the ruined roller coaster, so close
that the children had to walk along its edge to
reach the ivy-covered carts. The pit was not
very deep, although its walls were just high

enough that nobody could climb out if they were thrown inside, and it was not very large, so all the lions were as crowded together as they had been in the trailer. Like the Baudelaires' coworkers, the lions must not have had much to sleep on, and they were still dozing in the morning sun. Sound asleep, the lions did not look particularly ferocious. Some of their manes were all tangled, as if no one had brushed them for a long time, and sometimes one of their legs twitched, as if they were dreaming of better days. On their backs and bellies were several nasty scars from the whippings Count Olaf had given them, which made the Baudelaires sore just looking at them, and most of the lions were very, very thin, as if they had not eaten a good meal in quite some time.

"I feel sorry for them," Violet said, looking at one lion who was so skinny that all of its ribs were visible. "If Madame Lulu was right, these lions were once noble creatures, and now look how miserably Count Olaf has treated them."

"They look lonely," Klaus said, squinting down into the pit with a sad frown. "Maybe they're orphans, too."

"But maybe they have a surviving parent," Violet said, "somewhere in the Mortmain Mountains."

"Edasurc," Sunny said, which meant something like, "Maybe someday we can rescue these lions."

"For now, let's rescue ourselves," Violet said with a sigh. "Klaus, let's see if we can untangle the ivy from this cart in front. We'll probably need two carts, one for passengers and one for the archival library, so Sunny, see if you can get the ivy off that other one."

"Easy," said Sunny, pointing to her teeth.

"All the caravans are on wheels," Klaus said. "Would it be easier to hitch up one of the caravans to the lightning device?"

"A caravan is too big," Violet replied. "If you wanted to move a caravan, you'd have to attach it to an automobile, or several horses.

We'll be lucky if I can rebuild the carts' engines. Madame Lulu said that they were rusted away."

"It seems like we're hitching our hopes to a risky plan," Klaus said, tearing away at a few strands of ivy with the one arm he could use. "But I suppose it's no more risky than plenty of other things we've done, like stealing a sailboat."

"Or climbing up an elevator shaft," Violet said.

"Whaque," Sunny said, with her mouth full of plants, and her siblings knew she meant something along the lines of, "Or pretending to be surgeons."

"Actually," Violet said, "maybe this plan isn't so risky after all. Look at the axles on this cart."

"Axles?" Klaus asked.

"The rods that hold the wheels in place," she explained, pointing to the bottom of the cart. "They're in perfect condition. That's good news, because we need these wheels to carry us a long way." The eldest Baudelaire looked up from her work and gazed out at the horizon. To the east, the sun was rising, and soon its rays would reflect off the mirrors positioned in the fortune-telling tent, but to the north, she could see the Mortmain Mountains rising up in odd, square shapes, more like a staircase than a mountain range, with patches of snow on the higher places, and the top steps covered in a thick, gray fog. "It'll take a long time to get up there," she said, "and it doesn't look like there are a lot of repair shops on the way."

"I wonder what we'll find up there," Klaus said. "I've never been to the headquarters of something."

"Neither have I," Violet said. "Here, Klaus, lean down with me so I can look at the engine of this cart."

"If we knew more about V.F.D.," Klaus said, "we might know what to expect. How does the engine look?"

"Not too bad," Violet said. "Some of these

pistons are completely rusted away, but I think I can replace them with these latches on the sides of the cart, and the lightning device will provide a fan belt. But we'll need something else—something like twine, or wire, to help connect the two carts."

"Ivy?" Sunny asked.

"Good idea, Sunny," Violet said. "The stems of the ivy feel solid enough. If you'll pluck the leaves off a few strands, you'd be a big help."

"What can I do?" Klaus asked.

"Help me turn the cart over," Violet said, "but watch where you put your feet. We don't want you falling into the pit."

"I don't want *anyone* falling into the pit," Klaus said. "You don't think the others will throw Madame Lulu to the lions, do you?"

"Not if we get this done in time," Violet said grimly. "See if you can help me bend the latch so it fits into that notch, Klaus. No, no—the *other* way. I just hope Esmé doesn't have them throw somebody else in when we all escape."

"She probably will," Klaus said, struggling with the latch. "I can't understand why Hugo, Colette, and Kevin want to join up with people who do such things."

"I guess they're just happy that anybody's treating them like normal people," Violet said, and glanced into the pit. One of the lions yawned, stretched its paws, and opened one sleepy eye, but seemed uninterested in the three children working nearby. "Maybe that's why the hook-handed man works for Count Olaf, or the bald man with the long nose. Maybe when they tried to work someplace else, everyone laughed at them."

"Or maybe they just like committing crimes," Klaus said.

"That's a possibility, too," Violet said, and then frowned at the bottom of the cart. "I wish I had Mother's tool kit," she said. "She had this tiny wrench I always admired, and it would be just perfect for this job."

"She'd probably be a better help than I am," Klaus said. "I can't make head or tail of what you're doing."

"You're doing fine," Violet said, "particularly if you consider that we're sharing a shirt. How are those ivy stems coming, Sunny?"

"Lesoint," Sunny replied, which meant "I'm nearly done."

"Good work," Violet said, peering at the sun. "I'm not sure how much time we have. Count Olaf is probably inside the fortune-telling tent by now, asking the crystal ball about our whereabouts. I hope Madame Lulu keeps her promise, and doesn't give him what he wants. Will you hand me that piece of metal on the ground, Klaus? It looks like it used to be part of the tracks, but I'm going to use it to make a steering device."

"I wish Madame Lulu could give us what *we* want," Klaus said, handing the piece to his sister. "I wish we could find out if one of our parents survived the fire, without wandering around a mountain range."

"Me, too," Violet said, "and even then we might not find them. They could be down here looking for us."

"Remember the train station?" Klaus said, and Violet nodded.

"Esoobac," Sunny asked, handing over the ivy stems. By "Esoobac," she meant something like, "I don't remember," although there was no way she could have, as the youngest Baudelaire hadn't been born at the time her siblings were remembering. The Baudelaire family had decided to go away for the weekend to a vineyard, a word which here means "a sort of farm where people grow grapes used in wine." This vineyard was famous for having grapes that smelled delicious, and it was very pleasant to picnic in the fields, while the fragrance drifted in the air and the vineyard's famous donkeys, who helped carry bushels of grapes at harvesttime, slept in the shade of the grapevines. To reach the vineyard, the Baudelaires had to take not one train but two, transferring at a busy station not far from Paltryville, and on the day that Violet and Klaus were remembering, the children had been separated from their parents in the rush of the transferring crowd. Violet and Klaus, who were quite young, decided to search for their parents in the row of shops just outside the station, and soon the local shoemaker, blacksmith, chimney sweep, and computer technician were all helping the two frightened children look for their mother and father. Soon enough the Baudelaire family was reunited, but the children's father had taught them a serious lesson. "If you lose us," he said, "stay put."

"Yes," their mother agreed. "Don't go wandering around looking for us. *We'll* come and find *you*."

At the time, Violet and Klaus had solemnly agreed, but times had changed. When the Baudelaire parents had said "If you lose us," they were referring to times when the children might lose sight of them in a crowd, as they had at the train station that day, where I had lunch just a few weeks ago and talked to the shoe-maker's son about what had happened. They were not referring to the way the Baudelaires had lost them now, in a deadly fire that it seemed had claimed at least one of their lives. There are times to stay put, and what you want will come to you, and there are times to go out into the world and find such a thing for your-self. Like the Baudelaire orphans, I have found myself in places where staying put would be dangerously foolish, and foolishly dangerous. I have stood in a department store, and seen something written on a price tag that told me I had to leave at once, but in different clothing. I have sat in an airport, and heard something over the loudspeaker that told me I had to leave later that day, but on a different flight. And I have stood alongside the roller coaster at Cali-gari Carnival, and known what the Baudelaires could not possibly have known that quiet morn-ing. I have looked at the carts, all melted

together and covered in ash, and I have gazed
into the pit dug by Count Olaf and his henchmen and seen all the burnt bones lying in a
heap, and I have picked through the bits of mirror and crystal where the fortune-telling tent
once stood, and all this research has told me the
same thing, and if somehow I could slip back in
time, as easily as I could slip out of the disguise
I am in now, I would walk to the edge of that
pit and tell the Baudelaire orphans the results
of my findings. But of course I cannot. I can only
fulfill my sacred duty and type this story as best
I can, down to the last worf.

"Worf," Sunny said, when the Baudelaires
had finished telling her about the train station.
By "worf," she meant something along the lines
of, "I don't think we should stay put. I think we
should leave right now."

"We can't leave yet," Violet said. "The
steering device is ready, and the carts are firmly
attached to one another, but without a fan belt,
the engine won't work. We'd better go to the

fortune-telling tent and dismantle the lightning device."

"Olaf?" Sunny asked.

"Let's hope that Madame Lulu has sent him on his way," Violet said, "otherwise we'll be cutting it close. We have to finish our invention before the show begins, otherwise everyone will see us get in the carts and leave."

There was a faint growl from the pit, and the children saw that most of the lions were awake and looking around crankily at their surroundings. Some of them were trying to pace around their cramped quarters, but they only managed to get in the way of other lions, which only made them crankier.

"Those lions look hungry," Klaus said. "I wonder if it's almost show time."

"Aklec," Sunny said, which meant "Let's move out," and the Baudelaires moved out, walking away from the roller coaster and toward the fortune-telling tent. As the children walked through the carnival, they saw that quite a few visitors had already arrived, and some of them giggled at the siblings as they made their way.

"Look!" one man said, pointing at the Baudelaires with a sneer. "Freaks! Let's be sure to go to the lion show later—one of them might get eaten."

"Oh, I hope so," said his companion. "I didn't come all the way out here to the hinterlands for nothing."

"The woman at the ticket booth told me that a journalist from *The Daily Punctilio* is here to report on who gets devoured," said another man, who was wearing a CALIGARI CARNIVAL T-shirt he had apparently purchased at the gift caravan.

"*The Daily Punctilio*!" cried the woman who was with him. "How exciting! I've been reading about those Baudelaire murderers for weeks. I just love violence!"

"Who doesn't?" the man replied. "Especially when it's combined with sloppy eating."

Just as the Baudelaires reached the fortune-

telling tent, a man stepped in front of them and blocked their way. The children looked up at the pimples on his chin and recognized him as the very rude member of the audience at the House of Freaks.

"Why, look who's here," he said. "It's Chabo the Wolf Baby, and Beverly and Elliot, the two-headed freak."

"It's very nice to see you again," Violet said quickly. She tried to walk around him, but he grabbed the shirt she was sharing with her brother, and she had to stop so he wouldn't tear the shirt and reveal their disguise.

"What about your other head?" the pimpled man asked sarcastically. "Doesn't he think it's nice to see me?"

"Of course," Klaus said, "but we're in a bit of a hurry, so if you'll excuse us . . ."

"I don't excuse freaks," the man said. "There's no excuse for them. Why don't you wear a sack over one of your heads, so you look normal?"

"Grr!" Sunny said, baring her teeth at the man's knees.

"Please leave us alone, sir," Violet said. "Chabo is very protective of us, and might bite you if you get too close."

"I bet Chabo's no match for a bunch of ferocious lions," the man said. "I can't wait until the show, and neither can my mother."

"That's right, dear," said a woman who was standing nearby. She stepped forward to give the pimpled man a big kiss, and the Baudelaires noticed that pimples seemed to run in the family. "What time does the show start, freaks?"

"The show starts right now!"

The pimpled man and his mother turned around to see who had spoken, but the Baudelaires did not have to look to know it was Count Olaf who had made the announcement. The villain was standing at the entrance to the fortune-telling tent with a whip in his hand and a particularly nasty gleam in his eye, both of which the siblings recognized. The whip, of course, was the one that Count Olaf used to encourage the lions to become ferocious, which the Baudelaires had seen the previous day, and the gleam was something they had seen more times than they could count. It was the sort of gleam someone might get in their eye when they were telling a joke, but when Olaf looked at people that way it usually meant that one of his schemes was succeeding brilliantly.

"The show starts right now!" he announced again to the people gathering around him. "I've just had my fortune told, so I've gotten what I wanted." Count Olaf pointed at the fortune-telling tent with his whip, and then turned around to point at the disguised Baudelaires as he grinned at the crowd. "Now, ladies and gentlemen, it's time to go to the lion pit so we can give the rest of you what you want."

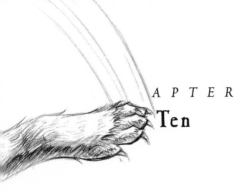

"I'm going to the pit right now!" cried a woman in the crowd. "I want to have a good view of the show!"

"So do I," said a man standing next to her. "There's no point in having lions eat somebody if you can't watch it happen."

"Well, we'd better hurry," said the man with pimples on his chin. "There's quite a crowd here."

The Baudelaire orphans looked around and saw that the pimpled man was speaking the truth.

News of Caligari Carnival's latest

C

H

attraction must have spread far beyond the hinterlands, because there were many more visitors than yesterday, and there seemed to be more and more arriving every minute.

"I'll lead the way to the pit," announced Count Olaf. "After all, the lion show was my idea, so I should get to walk in front."

"It was your idea?" asked a woman the children recognized from their stay at Heimlich Hospital. She was wearing a gray suit, and chewing gum as she spoke into a microphone, and the siblings remembered that she was a reporter from *The Daily Punctilio*. "I'd love to write about it in the newspaper. What is your name?"

"Count Olaf!" Count Olaf said proudly.

"I can see the headline now: 'COUNT OLAF THINKS UP IDEA FOR LION SHOW,'" said the reporter. "Wait until the readers of *The Daily Punctilio* see that!"

"Wait a minute," someone said. "I thought Count Olaf was murdered by those three children."

"That was Count Omar," replied the reporter. "I should know. I've been writing about the Baudelaires for *The Daily Punctilio*. Count Omar was murdered by those three Baudelaire children, who still remain at large."

"Well, if anyone ever finds them," someone in the crowd said, "we'll throw *them* into the lion pit."

"An excellent idea," Count Olaf replied, "but in the meantime, the lions will have a meal of one delicious freak. Follow me, everyone, for an afternoon of violence and sloppy eating!"

"Hooray!" cried several members of the crowd, as Olaf took a bow and began to lead everyone in the direction of the ruined roller coaster where the lions were waiting.

"Come with me, freaks," Count Olaf ordered, pointing at the Baudelaires. "My assistants are bringing the others. We want all you freaks assembled for the choosing ceremony."

"I will bring them, my Olaf," Madame Lulu said in her disguised accent, emerging from the

fortune-telling tent. When she saw the Baudelaires, her eyes widened, and she quickly held
her hands behind her back. "You lead crowd to
pit, please, and give interview to newspaper on
way."

"Oh, yes," said the reporter. "I can see the
headline now: 'EXCLUSIVE INTERVIEW WITH
COUNT OLAF, WHO IS NOT COUNT OMAR, WHO IS
DEAD.' Wait until the readers of *The Daily Punctilio* see that!"

"It will be exciting for people to read about
me," Count Olaf said. "All right, I'll walk with
the reporter, Lulu. But hurry up with the freaks."

"Yes, my Olaf," Madame Lulu said. "Come
with me, freaky peoples, please."

Lulu held out her hands for the Baudelaires
to take, as if she were their mother walking
them across the street, instead of a fake fortune-
teller leading them to a pit of lions. The children could see that one of Madame Lulu's
palms had an odd streak of dirt on it, while the
other hand was closed in an odd, tight fist. The

children did not want to take those hands and walk toward the lion show, but there were so many people gathered around, eagerly expecting violence, that it seemed they had no other choice. Sunny grabbed ahold of Lulu's right hand, and Violet grabbed Lulu's left, and they walked together in an awkward knot in the direction of the ruined roller coaster.

"Olivi—" Klaus started to say, but then looked around the crowd and realized it would be foolish to use her real name. "I mean, Madame Lulu," he corrected himself, and then leaned across Violet to speak as quietly as he could. "Let's walk as slowly as we can. Maybe we can find an opportunity to sneak back to the tent and dismantle the lightning device."

Madame Lulu did not answer, but merely shook her head slightly to indicate that it was not a good time to speak of such matters.

"Fan belt," Sunny reminded her, as quietly as she could, but Madame Lulu just shook her head.

"You kept your promise, didn't you?" Klaus murmured, scarcely above a whisper, but Madame Lulu stared ahead as if she had not heard. He nudged his older sister inside their shared shirt. "Violet," he said, scarcely daring to use her real name. "Ask Madame Lulu to walk more slowly."

Violet glanced briefly at Klaus, and then turned her head to catch Sunny's eye. The younger Baudelaires looked back at their sister and watched her shake her head slightly, just as Madame Lulu had, and then look down, where she was holding the fortune-teller's hand. Between two of Violet's fingers, Klaus and Sunny could see the tip of a small piece of rubber, which they recognized immediately. It was the part of Madame Lulu's lightning device that resembled a fan belt—the very thing Violet needed to turn the carts of the roller coaster into an invention that could carry the Baudelaires out of the hinterlands and up into the Mortmain Mountains. But instead of feeling hopeful as they looked at this crucial item in Violet's hand, all three Baudelaires felt something quite a bit less pleasant.

If you have ever experienced something that feels strangely familiar, as if the exact same thing has happened to you before, then you are experiencing what the French call "déjà vu." Like most French expressions—"ennui," which is a fancy term for severe boredom, or "la petite mort," which describes a feeling that part of you has died—"déjà vu" refers to something that is usually not very pleasant, and it was not pleasant for the Baudelaire orphans to arrive at the lion pit and experience the queasy feeling of déjà vu. When the children had been staying at Heimlich Hospital, they had found themselves in an operating theater, surrounded by a large crowd that was very eager to see something violent occur, such as an operation performed on someone. When the children were living in the town of V.F.D., they had found themselves in a field, surrounded by a large crowd eager to see something violent occur, such as the burning of someone at the stake. And now, as Madame Lulu let go of their hands, the children looked at the enormous and strangely familiar crowd towering over them at the ruined roller coaster. Once again, there were people eager for something violent to happen. Once again, the Baudelaires were afraid for their lives. And once again, it was all because of Count Olaf. The siblings looked past the cheering crowd at the two roller-coaster carts that Violet had adapted. All the invention needed was the fan belt, and the children could continue their search for one of the Baudelaire parents, but as Violet, Klaus, and Sunny looked across the pit at the two small carts joined with ivy and altered to travel across the hinterlands, they felt the queasiness of déjà vu and wondered if there was another unhappy ending in store for them.

"Welcome, ladies and gentlemen, to the most exciting afternoon of your entire lives!"

Count Olaf announced, and cracked his whip into the pit. The whip was just long enough to strike the restless lions, who roared obediently and gnashed their teeth in hunger. "These carnivorous lions are ready to eat a freak," he said. "But which freak will it be?"

The crowd parted, and the hook-handed man emerged, leading the Baudelaires' co-workers in a line toward the edge of the pit where the Baudelaires stood. Hugo, Colette, and Kevin had evidently been told to dress in their freakish clothes rather than in the gifts Esmé had given them, and they gave the Baudelaires a small smile and stared nervously at the snarling lions. Once the children's co-workers had taken their places, Count Olaf's other comrades emerged from the crowd. Esmé Squalor was wearing a pinstripe suit and carrying a parasol, which is a small umbrella used for keeping the sun out of one's eyes, and she smiled at the crowd and sat down on a small chair brought by Olaf's bald associate, who was also holding a long, flat piece of wood that he placed at the edge of the pit so it hung over the lions like a diving board over a swimming pool. Finally, the two white-faced women stepped forward, holding a small wooden box with a hole in the top.

"I'm so glad this is my last day in these clothes," Hugo murmured to the Baudelaires, gesturing to his ill-fitting coat. "Just think— soon I'll be a member of Count Olaf's troupe, and I'll never have to look like a freak again."

"Unless you're thrown to the lions," Klaus couldn't help replying.

"Are you kidding?" Hugo whispered back. "If I'm the one chosen, I'm going to throw Madame Lulu into the pit, just like Esmé said."

"Look closely at all these freaks," Count Olaf said, as several people in the audience tittered. "Observe Hugo's funny back. Think about how silly it is that Colette can bend herself into all sorts of strange positions. Giggle at the absurdity of Kevin's ambidextrous arms and legs. Snicker at Beverly and Elliot, the two-headed freak. And laugh so hard that you can scarcely breathe at Chabo the Wolf Baby."

The crowd erupted into laughter, pointing and laughing at the people they thought were funniest.

"Look at Chabo's ridiculous teeth!" cried a woman who had dyed her hair several colors at once. "She looks positively idiotic!"

"I think Kevin is funnier!" replied her husband, who had dyed his hair to match. "I hope he's thrown into the pit. It'll be fun to see him try to defend himself with both hands and feet."

"I hope it's the hook-handed freak!" said a woman standing in back of the Baudelaires. "That will make it even more violent!"

"I'm *not* a freak," the hook-handed man snarled impatiently. "I'm an employee of Count Olaf's."

"Oh, sorry," the woman replied. "In that case, I hope it's that man with pimples all over his chin."

"I'm a member of the audience!" the man cried. "I'm not a freak. I just have a few skin problems."

"Then what about that woman in that silly suit?" she asked. "Or that guy with only one eyebrow?"

"I'm Count Olaf's girlfriend," Esmé said, "and my suit is in, not silly."

"I don't care who's a freak and who isn't," said someone else in the crowd. "I just want to see the lions eat somebody."

"You will," Count Olaf promised. "We're going to have the choosing ceremony right now. The names of all the freaks have been written down on small scraps of paper and placed in the box that these two lovely ladies are holding."

The two white-faced women held up the wooden box and curtsied to the audience, while Esmé frowned at them. "I don't think they're particularly lovely," she said, but few people heard her over the cheering of the crowd.

"I'm going to reach inside the box," Count

Olaf said, "draw out one piece of paper, and read the name of the freak out loud. Then that freak will walk down that wooden plank and jump into the pit, and we'll all watch as the lions eat him."

"Or her," Esmé said. She looked over at Madame Lulu, and then at the Baudelaires and their coworkers. Putting down her parasol for a moment, she raised both of her long-nailed hands and made a small, pushing motion to remind them of her scheme.

"Or her," Count Olaf said, looking curiously at Esmé's gesture. "Now, are there any questions before we begin?"

"Why do you get to choose the name?" asked the pimpled man.

"Because this whole thing was my idea," Count Olaf said.

"I have a question," asked the woman with dyed hair. "Is this legal?"

"Oh, stop spoiling the fun," her husband said. "You wanted to come and watch people get eaten by lions, and so I brought you. If you're going to ask a bunch of complicated questions you can go wait in the car."

"Please continue, Your Countship," said the reporter from *The Daily Punctilio.*

"I will," Count Olaf said, and whipped the lions one more time before reaching into the wooden box. Giving the children and their coworkers a cruel smile, he moved his hand around inside the box for quite some time before at last drawing out a small piece of paper that had been folded many times. The crowd leaned forward to watch, and the Baudelaires strained to see over the heads of the adults around them. But Count Olaf did not unfold the piece of paper immediately. Instead he held it up as high as he could and gave the audience a large smile.

"I'm going to open the piece of paper very slowly," he announced, "to increase the suspense."

"How clever!" the reporter said, snapping

her gum in excitement. "I can see the headline now: 'COUNT OLAF INCREASES SUSPENSE.'"

"I learned how to amaze crowds by working extensively as a famous actor," Count Olaf said, smiling at the reporter and still holding up the piece of paper. "Be sure to write that down."

"I will," the reporter said breathlessly, and held her microphone closer to Olaf's mouth.

"Ladies and gentlemen," Count Olaf cried. "I am now unfolding the first fold in the piece of paper!"

"Oh boy!" cried several members of the audience. "Hooray for the first fold!"

"There are only five folds left," Olaf said. "Only five more folds, and we'll know which freak will be thrown to the lions."

"This is so exciting!" cried the man with dyed hair. "I might faint!"

"Just don't faint into the pit," his wife said.

"I am now unfolding the second fold in the piece of paper!" Count Olaf announced. "Now there are only four folds left!"

The lions roared impatiently, as if they were tired of all this nonsense with the piece of paper, but the audience cheered for the increased suspense and paid no attention to the beasts in the pit, gazing only at Count Olaf, who smiled and blew kisses to the carnival visitors. The Baudelaires, however, were no longer looking over the heads of the crowd to watch Olaf do his shtick, a phrase which here means "increase suspense by slowly unfolding a piece of paper printed with the name of someone who was supposed to jump into a pit of lions." They were taking advantage of the fact that no one was watching them, and stepped as close as they could to one another so they could talk without being overheard.

"Do you think we could sneak around the pit to the roller-coaster carts?" Klaus murmured to his sister.

"I think it's too crowded," Violet replied. "Do you think we could get the lions not to eat anyone?"

"I think they're too hungry," Klaus said, squinting down at the growling beasts. "I read a book about large feline animals that said if they're hungry enough, they'll eat practically anything."

"Is there anything else you've read about lions that can help us?" Violet asked.

"I don't think so," Klaus replied. "Is there anything else you can invent from that fan belt that can help us?"

"I don't think so," Violet replied, her voice faint with fear.

"Déjà vu!" Sunny called up to her siblings. She meant something along the lines of, "We must be able to think of something that can help us. We've escaped from bloodthirsty crowds before."

"Sunny's right," Klaus said. "When we lived at Heimlich Hospital, we learned about stalling a crowd, when we postponed Olaf's scheme to operate on you."

"And when we lived at the Village of Fowl

Devotees," Violet said, "we learned about mob psychology, when we watched all the villagers get so upset that they couldn't think clearly. But what can we do with this crowd? What can we do now?"

"Both!" Sunny murmured, and then growled quickly in case anybody was listening.

"I unfolded the paper again!" Count Olaf crowed, and I probably do not have to tell you that he explained that there were only three folds left, or that the crowd cheered him once more, as if he had done something very brave or very noble. I probably do not have to tell you that he announced the remaining three folds as if they were very exciting events, and that the crowd cheered him each time, eagerly awaiting the violence and sloppy eating that would follow, and I probably don't even have to tell you what was written on the piece of paper, because if you have read this far in this wretched book then you are well acquainted with the Baudelaire orphans and you know what kind of freakish luck they have. A person with normal luck would arrive at a carnival in comfortable circumstances, such as in a double-decker bus or on the back of an elephant, and would probably have a pleasant time enjoying all of the things a carnival has to offer, and would feel happy and content at the end of their stay. But the Baudelaires had arrived at Caligari Carnival in the trunk of an automobile, and had been forced to put themselves in uncomfortable disguises, take part in a humiliating show, and place themselves in dangerous circumstances, and, as their freakish luck would have it, had not even found the information they were hoping to discover. So it probably will not be a surprise to you to learn that Hugo's name was not printed on the piece of paper in Count Olaf's hand, or Colette's name, or the name of Kevin, who was clasping his equally skilled hands together in nervousness as Olaf finally unfolded the paper completely. It will not surprise you that when Count Olaf announced what the paper said, the eyes of the entire crowd fell on the disguised children. But although you might not be surprised at Count Olaf's announcement, you might be surprised at the announcement that one of the siblings made immediately afterward.

"Ladies and gentlemen," Count Olaf announced, "Beverly and Elliot, the two-headed freak, will be thrown to the lions today."

"Ladies and gentlemen," Violet Baudelaire announced, "we are thrilled to be chosen."

C H A P T E R
Eleven

There is another writer I know, who, like myself, is thought by a great deal of people to be dead. His name is William Shakespeare, and he has written four kinds of plays: comedies, romances, histories, and tragedies. Comedies, of course, are stories in which people tell jokes and trip over things, and romances are stories in which people fall in love and probably get married. Histories are retellings of things that actually happened,

like my history of the Baudelaire orphans, and tragedies are stories that usually begin fairly happily and then steadily go downhill, until all of the characters are dead, wounded, or otherwise inconvenienced. It is usually not much fun to watch a tragedy, whether you are in the audience or one of the characters, and out of all Shakespeare's tragedies possibly the least fun example is *King Lear,* which tells the story of a king who goes mad while his daughters plot to murder one another and other people who are getting on their nerves. Toward the end of the play, one of William Shakespeare's characters remarks that "Humanity must perforce prey upon itself, like monsters of the deep," a sentence which here means "How sad it is that people end up hurting one another as if they were ferocious sea monsters," and when the character utters those unhappy words, the people in Shakespeare's audience often weep, or sigh, or remind themselves to see a comedy next time.

I am sorry to report that the story of the

Baudelaire orphans has reached a point where it is appropriate to borrow Mr. Shakespeare's rather depressing sentence to describe how the Baudelaire orphans felt as they addressed the crowd gathered at the edge of the lion pit and tried to continue the story they found themselves in without turning it into a tragedy, when it seemed that everyone was eager to hurt one another. Count Olaf and his henchmen were eager to see Violet and Klaus jump to their carnivorous deaths, so that Caligari Carnival would become more popular, and Madame Lulu would continue telling Olaf's fortune. Esmé Squalor was eager to see Madame Lulu thrown into the pit, so that she could get all of Olaf's attention, and the Baudelaires' coworkers were eager to help, so they could join Olaf's troupe. The reporter from *The Daily Punctilio* and the other members of the audience were eager to see violence and sloppy eating, so their visit to the carnival would be worthwhile, and the lions were eager for a meal, after being whipped and denied food for so long. It seemed that every member of humanity gathered at the roller coaster that afternoon was eager for something awful to occur, and the children felt awful as Violet and Klaus stepped toward the plank and pretended they were just as eager.

"Thank you, Count Olaf, for choosing my other head and I as the first victims in the lion show," Klaus said grandly in his high-pitched voice.

"Um, you're welcome," Count Olaf replied, looking a bit surprised. "Now, jump into the pit so we can watch the lions devour you."

"And do it quickly!" cried the man with pimples on his chin. "I'd like my carnival visit to be worthwhile!"

"Instead of watching a freak jump into the pit," Violet said, thinking quickly, "wouldn't you rather watch someone push a freak into the pit? That would be much more violent."

"Grr!" Sunny growled, in disguised agreement.

"That's a good point," one of the white-faced women said thoughtfully.

"Oh yes!" cried the woman with dyed hair. "I want to see the two-headed freak thrown to the lions!"

"I agree," Esmé said, glaring at the two older Baudelaires and then at Madame Lulu. "I'd like to see someone thrown into the pit."

The crowd cheered and applauded, and Sunny watched as her two siblings took a step toward the plank that hung over the pit where the lions were waiting hungrily. There are tiresome people who say that if you ever find yourself in a difficult situation, you should stop and figure out the right thing to do, but the three siblings already knew that the right thing to do was to dash over to the roller-coaster carts, hook up the fan belt, and escape into the hinterlands with Madame Lulu and her archival library, after calmly explaining to the gathered crowd that bloodshed was not a proper form of entertainment and that Count Olaf and his troupe ought to be arrested that very instant. But there are times in this harum-scarum world when figuring out the right thing to do is quite simple, but doing the right thing is simply impossible, and then you must do something else. The three Baudelaires, standing in their disguises in the midst of a crowd eager for violence and sloppy eating, knew that they could not do the right thing, but they thought they could try to get the crowd as frantic as possible, so that they might slip away in the confusion. Violet, Klaus, and Sunny weren't sure if using the techniques of stalling and mob psychology was the right thing to do, but the Baudelaire orphans could not think of anything else, and whether or not it was the right thing to do, their plan did seem to be working.

"This is absolutely thrilling!" exclaimed the reporter excitedly. "I can see the headline now: 'FREAKS PUSHED INTO LION PIT!' Wait until the readers of *The Daily Punctilio* see that!"

Sunny made the loudest growl she could, and pointed one of her tiny fingers at Count

Olaf. "What Chabo is trying to convey in her half-wolf language," Klaus said, "is that Count Olaf ought to be the one to push us into the pit. After all, the lion show was his idea."

"That's true!" the pimpled man said. "Let's see Olaf throw Beverly and Elliot into the pit!"

Count Olaf scowled at the Baudelaires, and then gave the crowd a smile that showed quite a few of his filthy teeth. "I am deeply honored to be asked," he said, bowing slightly, "but I'm afraid it would not be appropriate at this time."

"Why not?" demanded the woman with dyed hair.

Count Olaf paused for a moment, and then made a short, high-pitched sound as disguised as Sunny's growl. "I'm allergic to cats," he explained. "You see? I'm sneezing already, and I'm not even on the plank."

"Your allergies didn't bother you when you were whipping the lions," Violet said.

"That's true," the hook-handed man said. "I didn't even know you had allergies, Olaf."

Count Olaf glared at his henchman. "Ladies and gentlemen," he began, but the crowd didn't want to hear another one of the villain's speeches.

"Push the freak in, Olaf!" someone shouted, and everyone cheered. Count Olaf frowned, but grabbed Klaus's hand and led the two eldest Baudelaires onto the plank. But as the crowd roared around them and the lions roared beneath them, the Baudelaires could see that Count Olaf was no more eager to get any closer to the hungry lions than they were.

"Throwing people into pits isn't really my job," Count Olaf said nervously to the crowd. "I'm more of an actor."

"I have an idea," Esmé said suddenly, in a false sweet voice, "Madame Lulu, why don't you walk down that plank and throw your freak to its death?"

"This is not really my job either, please," Madame Lulu protested, looking at the children nervously. "I am fortune-teller, not freak-thrower."

"Don't be so modest, Madame Lulu," Count Olaf said with a nasty smile. "Even though the lion show was my idea, you're the most important person here at the carnival. Take my place on the plank, so we can see someone get pushed to their death."

"What a nice offer!" the reporter cried. "You're a very generous person, Count Olaf!"

"Let's see Madame Lulu throw Beverly and Elliot into the pit!" cried the pimpled man, and everyone cheered again. As mob psychology began to take hold, the crowd seemed to be as flexible as it was excited, and they gave the fortune-teller an enormous round of applause as she nervously took Count Olaf's place on the plank. The piece of wood teetered for a moment from the weight of so many people standing on it, and the older Baudelaires had to struggle to keep their balance. The crowd gasped in excitement, and then groaned as the two disguised children managed not to fall.

"This is so exciting!" squealed the reporter. "Maybe Lulu will fall in, too!"

"Yes," Esmé snarled. "Maybe she will."

"I don't care who falls in!" announced the pimpled man. Frustrated by the delay in violence and sloppy eating, he tossed his cold beverage into the pit and splashed several lions, who roared in annoyance. "To me, a woman in a turban is just as freaky as a two-headed person. I'm not prejudiced!"

"Me neither!" agreed someone who was wearing a hat with the words CALIGARI CARNIVAL printed on it. "I'm just eager for this show to finally get started! I hope Madame Lulu is brave enough to push that freak in!"

"It doesn't matter if she's brave enough," the bald man replied with a chuckle. "Everyone will do what they're expected to do. What other choice do they have?"

Violet and Klaus had reached the end of the plank, and they tried as hard as they could to think of an answer to the bald man's question.

Below them was a roaring mass of hungry lions, who had gathered so closely together below the wooden board that they just seemed to be a mass of waving claws and open mouths, and around them was a roaring crowd of people who were watching them with eager smiles on their faces. The Baudelaires had succeeded in getting the crowd more and more frantic, but they still hadn't found an opportunity to slip away in the confusion, and now it seemed like that opportunity would never knock. With difficulty, Violet turned her head to face her brother, and Klaus squinted back at her, and Sunny could see that her siblings' eyes were filled with tears.

"Our luck may have run out," she said.

"Stop whispering to your heads!" Count Olaf ordered in a terrible voice. "Madame Lulu, push them in this instant"

"We're increasing the suspense!" Klaus cried back desperately.

"The suspense has been increased enough,"

replied the man with the pimpled chin impatiently. "I'm getting tired of all this stalling!"

"Me, too!" cried the woman with dyed hair.

"Me, too!" cried someone else standing nearby. "Olaf, hit Lulu with the whip! That'll get her to stop stalling!"

"Just one moment, please," Madame Lulu said, and took another step toward Violet and Klaus. The plank teetered again, and the lions roared, hoping that their lunch was about to arrive. Madame Lulu looked at the elder Baudelaires frantically and the children saw her shoulders shrug slightly underneath her shimmering robe.

"Enough of this!" the hook-handed man said, and stepped forward impatiently. "I'll throw them in myself. I guess I'm the only person here brave enough to do it!"

"Oh, no," Hugo said. "I'm brave enough, too, and so are Colette and Kevin."

"Freaks who are brave?" the hook-handed man sneered. "Don't be ridiculous!"

"We *are* brave," Hugo insisted. "Count Olaf, let us prove it to you, and then you can employ us!"

"Employ you?" Count Olaf asked with a frown.

"What a wonderful idea!" Esmé exclaimed, as if the idea had not been hers.

"Yes," Colette said. "We'd like to find something else to do, and this seems like a wonderful opportunity."

Kevin stepped forward and held out both his hands. "I know I'm a freak," he said to Olaf, "but I think I could be just as useful as the hook-handed man, or your bald associate."

"What?" the bald man snapped. "A freak like you, as useful as me? Don't be ridiculous!"

"I can be useful," Kevin insisted. "You just watch."

"Stop all this bickering!" the pimpled man said crankily. "I didn't visit this carnival to hear people argue about their work problems."

"You're distracting me and my other head,"

Violet said in her low, disguised voice. "Let's get off this plank and we can all discuss this matter calmly."

"I don't want to discuss things calmly!" cried the woman with dyed hair. "I can do that at home!"

"Yes!" agreed the reporter from *The Daily Punctilio*. "'PEOPLE DISCUSS THINGS CALMLY' is a boring headline! Somebody throw somebody else into the lion pit, and we'll all get what we want!"

"Madame Lulu will do it, please!" Madame Lulu announced in a booming voice, and grabbed Violet and Klaus by the shirt. The Baudelaires looked up at her and saw a tear appear in one of her eyes, and she leaned down to speak to them. "I'm sorry, Baudelaires," she murmured quietly, without a trace of accent, and reached down to Violet's hand and took the fan belt away from her.

Sunny was so upset that she forgot to growl. "Trenceth!" she shrieked, which meant something along the lines of, "You ought to be ashamed of yourself!" but if the fake fortune-teller was ashamed of herself she did not behave accordingly. "Madame Lulu always says you must always give people what they want," she said grandly in her disguised voice. "She will do the throwing, please, and she will do it now!"

"Don't be ridiculous," Hugo said, stepping forward eagerly. "I'll do it!"

"You're the one being ridiculous!" Colette said, contorting her body toward Lulu. "I'll do it!"

"No, I'll do it!" Kevin cried. "With both hands!"

"*I'll* do it!" the bald man cried, blocking Kevin's way. "I don't want a freak like you for a coworker!"

"I'll do it!" cried the hook-handed man.

"I'll do it!" cried one of the white-faced women.

"I'll do it!" cried the other one.

"I'll get someone else to do it!" cried Esmé Squalor.

Count Olaf unwound his whip and flicked

it over the heads of the crowd with a mighty *snap!* that made everyone cower, a word which here means "cringe and duck and hope not to get whipped." *"Silence!"* he commanded in a terrible roar. "All of you ought to be ashamed of yourselves. You're arguing like a bunch of children! I want to see those lions devouring someone this very instant, and whoever has the courage to carry out my orders will get a special reward!"

This speech, of course, was just the latest example of Count Olaf's tedious philosophy concerning a stubborn mule moving in the proper direction if there is a carrot dangling in front of it, but the offer of a special reward finally got the crowd as frantic as possible. In a moment, the crowd of carnival visitors had become a mob of volunteers, all of whom swarmed eagerly forward to finally throw someone to the lions. Hugo lunged forward to push Madame Lulu, but bumped into the box that the white-faced women were holding, and the three of them fell in a heap at the edge of the pit. The hook-handed man lunged forward to grab Violet and Klaus, but his hook caught in the cord of the reporter's microphone and became hopelessly entangled. Colette contorted her arms so as to grab Lulu's ankles, but grabbed Esmé Squalor's ankle by accident, and got her hands all twisted around one of Esmé's fashionable shoes. The woman with dyed hair decided she might give it a try, and leaned forward to push the elder Baudelaires, but they stepped to the side and the woman fell into her husband, who accidentally slapped the man with pimples on his chin, and the three carnival visitors began arguing loudly. Quite a few people who were standing nearby decided to get in on the argument, and gathered around to shout in each other's faces. Within moments of Count Olaf's announcement, the Baudelaires were in the middle of a furious mass of humanity, who were standing over the children, yelling and pushing and preying on themselves like monsters of the deep, while the lions roared furiously in the pit below.

But then the siblings heard another sound in the pit, a horrible crunching and ripping sound that was far worse than the roaring of beasts. The crowd stopped arguing to see what was making the noise, but the Baudelaires were not interested in seeing anything more, and stepped back from the terrible sound, and huddled against one another with their eyes shut as tightly as possible. Even in this position, however, the children could hear the terrible, terrible sounds from the pit, even over the laughter and cheers of the carnival visitors as they crowded together at the edge of the pit to see what was happening, and so the three youngsters turned away from the commotion, and, with their eyes still closed, slipped away in the confusion, stumbling through all of the cheering people until at last they were in the clear, a phrase which here means "far enough away from the roller coaster that they could no longer see or hear what was going on."

But the Baudelaire orphans, of course, could still imagine what was happening, as I can imagine it, even though I was not there that afternoon and have only read descriptions of what occurred down in the pit. The article in *The Daily Punctilio* says that it was Madame Lulu who fell first, but newspaper articles are often inaccurate, so it is impossible to say if this is actually true. Perhaps she did fall first, and the bald man fell after her, or perhaps Lulu managed to push the bald man in as she tried to escape his grasp, only to slip and join him in the pit just moments later. Or perhaps these two people were still struggling when the plank teetered one more time, and the lions reached both of them at the same time. It is likely that I will never know, just as I will probably never know the location of the fan belt, no matter how many times I return to Caligari Carnival to search for it. At first I thought that Madame Lulu dropped the strip of rubber on the ground near the pit, but I have searched the entire area with a shovel and a flashlight and found no sign of it, and none of the carnival visitors whose houses I have searched seem to have taken it home for a souvenir. Then I thought that perhaps the fan belt was thrown into the air during all the commotion, and perhaps landed up in the tracks of the roller coaster, but I have climbed over every inch without success. And there is, of course, the possibility that it has burned away, but lightning devices are generally made of a certain type of rubber that is difficult to burn, so that possibility seems remote. And so I must admit that I do not know for certain where the fan belt is, and, like knowing whether it was the bald man or Madame Lulu who fell first, that this may be information that will never come to me. But I can imagine that the small strip of rubber ended up in the same place as the woman who removed it from the lightning device and gave it to the Baudelaire orphans, only to snatch it back at the last minute, and in the same place as the associate of Olaf's who was so eager to get a special reward. If I close my eyes, as the Baudelaire orphans closed their eyes as they stumbled away from this unfortunate event, I can imagine that the fan belt, like the bald man and my former associate Olivia, fell into the pit that Olaf and his henchmen had dug, and ended up in the belly of the beast.

When the Baudelaire orphans finally opened their eyes, they found that they had stumbled to the entrance of Madame Lulu's fortune-telling tent, with the initials V.F.D. still staring out at them. Most of the carnival visitors had walked over to the lion pit to see the show, so the siblings were alone in the fading afternoon, and once again there was no one watching over them as they stood in front of the tent, trembling and crying quietly. The last time they had stood for so long at the tent's entrance, the decoration had seemed to change before their very eyes until they saw that it was not a painting of an eye, but the insignia of an organization that might help them. Now they stood and stared again, hoping that something would change before their very eyes until they saw what it was that they could do. But nothing seemed to change no matter how hard they looked. The carnival remained silent, and the afternoon continued to creep toward evening, and the insignia on the tent simply stared back at the weeping Baudelaires.

"I wonder where the fan belt is," Violet said finally. Her voice was faint and almost hoarse, but her tears had stopped at last. "I wonder if it fell to the ground, or was thrown onto the tracks of the roller coaster, or if it ended up—"

"How can you think about a fan belt at a time like this?" Klaus asked, although his voice was not angry. Like his sister, he was still trembling inside the shirt they shared, and felt very tired, as is often the case after a long cry.

"I don't want to think about anything else," Violet said. "I don't want to think about Madame Lulu and the lions, and I don't want to think about Count Olaf and the crowd, and I don't want to think about whether or not we did the right thing."

"Right," Sunny said gently.

"I agree," Klaus said. "We did the best we could."

"I'm not so sure," Violet replied. "I had the fan belt in my hand. It was all we needed to finish the invention and escape from this awful place."

"You couldn't finish the invention," Klaus said. "We were surrounded by a crowd of people who wanted to see someone thrown to the lions. It's not our fault that she fell in instead."

"And bald," Sunny added.

"But we made the crowd even more frantic," Violet said. "First we stalled the show, and then we used mob psychology to get them excited about throwing somebody into the pit."

"Count Olaf is the one who thought up this whole ghastly scheme," Klaus said. "What happened to Madame Lulu is his fault, not ours."

"We promised to take her with us," Violet insisted. "Madame Lulu kept her promise and didn't tell Count Olaf who we were, but we didn't keep ours."

"We tried," Klaus said. "We tried to keep ours."

"Trying's not good enough," Violet said. "Are we going to *try* to find one of our parents? Are we going to *try* to defeat Count Olaf?"

"Yes," Sunny said firmly, and wrapped her arms around Violet's leg. The eldest Baudelaire looked down at her sister and her eyes filled with tears.

"Why are we here?" she asked. "We thought we could put on disguises and get ourselves out of trouble, but we're worse off than when we began. We don't know what V.F.D. stands for. We don't know where the Snicket file is. And we don't know if one of our parents is really alive."

"There are some things we might not know," Klaus said, "but that doesn't mean we should give up. We can find out what we need to know. We can find out anything."

Violet smiled through her tears. "You sound like a researcher," she said.

The middle Baudelaire reached into his pocket and pulled out his glasses. "I *am* a researcher," he said, and stepped toward the entrance to the tent. "Let's get to work."

"Ghede!" Sunny said, which meant something like, "I almost forgot about the archival library!" and she followed her siblings through the flap in the tent.

As soon as the Baudelaire orphans stepped inside, they saw that Madame Lulu had made quite a few preparations for her escape with the children, and it made them very sad to think that she would never return to the fortune-telling tent to collect the things she had waiting for her. Her disguise kit was all packed up again, and waiting by the door so she could take it with her. There was a cardboard box standing next to the cupboard, filled with food that could be eaten on the journey. And laid out on the table, next to Madame Lulu's replacement crystal ball and various parts of the lightning device she had dismantled, was a large piece of paper that was badly torn and looked very old, but the Baudelaires saw at once that it could help them.

"It's a map," Violet said. "It's a map of the Mortmain Mountains. She must have had it among her papers."

Klaus put his glasses on and peered at it closely. "Those mountains must be very cold this time of year," he said. "I didn't realize the altitude was so high."

"Never mind the altitude," Violet said. "Can you find the headquarters Lulu was talking about?"

"Let's see," Klaus said. "There's a star next to Plath Pass, but the key says that a star indicates a campground."

"Key?" Sunny asked.

"This chart in the corner of the map is called

a key," Klaus explained. "You see? The map-maker explains what each symbol means, so the map doesn't get too cluttered."

"There's a black rectangle there in the Richter Range," she said. "See? Over in the east?"

"A black rectangle indicates hibernation grounds," Klaus said. "There must be quite a few bears in the Mortmain Mountains. Look, there are five hibernation grounds near Silent Springs, and a large cluster of them at the top of Paucity Peak."

"And here," Violet said, "in the Valley of Four Drafts, where it looks like Madame Lulu spilled coffee."

"Valley of Four Drafts!" Klaus said.

"V.F.D.!" Sunny cried.

The Baudelaires peered together at the spot on the map. The Valley of Four Drafts was high up in the Mortmain Mountains, where it would be very cold. The Stricken Stream began there, and wound its way down to the sea in sagging curves through the hinterlands, and the map showed many, many hibernation grounds along the way. There was a small brown stain in the center of the valley, where four gaps in the mountains came together and where Lulu had probably spilled coffee, but there were no markings for a headquarters or for anything else.

"Do you think it means something?" Violet asked. "Or is it just a coincidence, like all the V.F.D.s we've come across?"

"I thought the V in V.F.D. stood for 'volunteer,'" Klaus said. "That's what we found written on a page of the Quagmire notebooks, and it's what Jacques Snicket said."

"Winnow?" Sunny asked, which meant "But where else could the headquarters be? There's no other marking on the map."

"Well, if V.F.D. is a secret organization," Violet said, "they might not put their headquarters on a map."

"Or it could be marked secretly," Klaus said, and leaned in to take a good look at the stain. "Maybe this isn't just a stain," he said. "Maybe it's a secret marking. Maybe Madame Lulu put some coffee here on purpose, so she could find the headquarters, but nobody else could."

"I guess we'll have to travel there," Violet said with a sigh, "and find out."

"How are we going to travel there?" Klaus said. "We don't know where the fan belt is."

"We might be missing some parts," Violet replied, "but that doesn't mean we should give up. I can build something else."

"You sound like an inventor," he said.

Violet smiled, and took her hair ribbon out of her pocket. "I *am* an inventor," she said. "I'll look around here and see if there's anything else we can use. Klaus, you look under the table at the archival library."

"We'd better get out of the clothes we're sharing," Klaus said, "or we can't do two things at once."

"Ingredi," Sunny said, which meant "Meanwhile, I'll look through all this food and make sure we have everything we need to prepare meals."

"Good idea," Violet said. "We'd better hurry before someone finds us."

"There you are!" called a voice from the entrance to the tent, and the Baudelaires jumped. Violet hurriedly stuffed her ribbon back into her pocket, and Klaus removed his glasses, so they could turn around without revealing their disguise. Count Olaf and Esmé Squalor were standing together in the doorway of the tent, with their arms around one another, looking tired but happy, as if they were two parents coming home after a long day at work, instead of a vicious villain and his scheming girlfriend coming into a fortune-teller's tent after an afternoon of violence. Esmé Squalor was clutching a small bouquet of ivy her boyfriend had apparently given her, and Count Olaf was holding a flaming torch, which was shining as brightly as his wicked eyes.

"I've been looking everywhere for you two," he said. "What are you doing in here?"

"We decided to let all of you freaks join us," Esmé said, "even though you weren't very courageous at the lions' pit."

"That's very kind of you to offer," Violet said quickly, "but you don't want cowards like us in your troupe."

"Sure we do," Count Olaf said, with a nasty smile. "We keep losing assistants, and it's always good to have a few to spare. I even asked the woman who runs the gift caravan to join us, but she was too worried about her precious figurines to know that opportunity was knocking."

"Besides," Esmé said, stroking Olaf's hair, "you don't really have any choice. We're going to burn this carnival down to eliminate all the evidence that we've been here. Most of the tents are already on fire, and the carnival visitors and carnival workers are running for their lives. If you don't join us, where can you possibly go?"

The Baudelaires looked at one another in dismay. "I guess you're right," Klaus said.

"Of course we're right," Esmé said. "Now get out of here and help us pack up the trunk."

"Wait a minute," Count Olaf said, and strode over to the table. "What's this?" he demanded. "It looks like a map."

"It *is* a map," Klaus admitted with a sigh, wishing he had hidden it in his pockets. "A map of the Mortmain Mountains."

"The Mortmain Mountains?" Count Olaf said, examining the map eagerly. "Why, that's where we're heading! Lulu said that if there was a parent alive, they'd be hiding up there! Does the map show any headquarters on it?"

"I think these black rectangles indicate headquarters," Esmé said, peering over Olaf's shoulder. "I'm pretty good at reading maps."

"No, they represent campgrounds," Olaf said, looking at the key, but then his face broke out into a smile. "Wait a minute," he said, and pointed to the stain the Baudelaires had been examining. "I haven't seen one of these in a long time," he said, stroking his scraggly chin.

"A small brown stain?" Esmé asked. "You saw that this morning."

"This is a coded stain," Count Olaf explained. "I was taught to use this on maps when I was a little boy. It's to mark a secret location without anyone else noticing."

"Except a smashing genius," Esmé said. "I guess we're heading for the Valley of Four Drafts."

"V.F.D.," Count Olaf said, and giggled. "That's appropriate. Well, let's go. Is there anything else useful in here?"

The Baudelaires looked quickly at the table, where the archival library was hidden. Underneath the black tablecloth decorated with silver stars was all the crucial information Madame Lulu had gathered to give her visitors what they wanted. The children knew that all sorts of important secrets could be found in the gathering of paper, and they shuddered to think what Count Olaf would do if he discovered all those secrets.

"No," Klaus said finally. "Nothing else useful."

Count Olaf frowned, and kneeled down so that his face was right next to Klaus's. Even without his glasses, the middle Baudelaire could see that Olaf had not washed his one eyebrow for quite some time, and could smell his breath as he spoke. "I think you're lying to me," the villain said, and waved the lit torch in Klaus's face.

"My other head is telling the truth," Violet said.

"Then what is that food doing there?" Count Olaf demanded, pointing at the cardboard box. "Don't you think food would be useful for a long journey?"

The Baudelaires sighed in relief. "Grr!" Sunny growled.

"Chabo compliments you on your cleverness," Klaus said, "and so do we. We hadn't noticed that box."

"That's why I'm the boss," Count Olaf said,

"because I'm smart and I have good eyesight."
He laughed nastily, and put the torch in Klaus's
hand. "Now then," he said, "I want you to light
this tent on fire, and then bring the box of food
over to the car. Chabo, come with me. I'm sure
I'll find something for you to sink your teeth
into."

"Grr," Sunny said doubtfully.

"Chabo would prefer to stay with us,"
Violet said.

"I couldn't care less what Chabo would prefer," Olaf snarled, and picked up the youngest
Baudelaire as if she were a watermelon. "Now
get busy."

Count Olaf and Esmé Squalor walked out of
the tent with Chabo, leaving the elder Baudelaires alone with the flaming torch.

"We'd better pick up the box first," Klaus
said, "and light the tent from the outside.
Otherwise we'll be surrounded by flames in no
time."

"Are we really going to follow Olaf's orders?"

Violet asked, looking at the table again. "The archival library might have the answers to all our questions."

"I don't think we have a choice," Klaus said. "Olaf is burning down the whole carnival, and riding with him is our only chance to get to the Mortmain Mountains. You don't have time to invent something, and I don't have time to look through the library."

"We could find one of the other carnival employees," Violet said, "and ask them if they would help us."

"Everyone either thinks that we're freaks or murderers," Klaus said. "Sometimes even I think so."

"If we join Count Olaf," Violet said, "we might become even more freakish and murderous."

"But if we don't join him," Klaus asked, "where can we possibly go?"

"I don't know," Violet said sadly, "but this can't be the right thing to do, can it?"

"Maybe it's harum-scarum," Klaus said, "like Olivia said."

"Maybe it is," Violet said, and walked awkwardly with her brother to the cardboard box and picked it up. Klaus held the torch, and the two Baudelaires walked out of the fortune-telling tent for the last time.

When they first stepped out, still wearing the same pair of pants, it seemed as if night had already fallen, although the air was black and not the blue of the famous hinterlands sunsets. But then Violet and Klaus realized that the air was filling with smoke. Looking around, they saw that many of the tents and caravans were already on fire, as Count Olaf had said, and the flames were billowing black smoke up into the sky. Around them, the last of the carnival visitors were rushing to escape from Olaf's treachery, and in the distance the siblings could hear the panicked roars of the lions, who were still trapped in the pit.

"This isn't the kind of violence I like!"

shouted the man with pimples on his face, coughing in the smoke as he ran by. "I prefer it when other people are in danger!"

"Me, too!" said the reporter from *The Daily Punctilio*, running alongside him. "Olaf told me that the Baudelaires are responsible! I can see the headline now: 'BAUDELAIRES CONTINUE THEIR LIVES OF CRIME!'"

"What kind of children would do such a terrible thing?" asked the man with the pimpled chin, but Violet and Klaus could not hear the answer over the voice of Count Olaf.

"Hurry up, you two-headed freak!" he called from around the corner. "If you don't come here right this minute, we're leaving without you!"

"Grr!" Sunny growled frantically, and at the sound of their baby sister's disguised voice, the older Baudelaires threw the lit torch into the fortune-telling tent, and ran toward Olaf's voice without looking back, although it wouldn't have mattered if they had looked. There was so much fire and smoke around them one more burning tent wouldn't have made the carnival look any different. The only difference was that they would have known that part of the fire was of their own devising, a phrase which here means "because of their part in Count Olaf's treachery," and although neither Violet nor Klaus saw this with their own eyes, they knew it in their hearts, and I doubt that they would ever forget it.

When the older Baudelaires rounded the corner, they saw that all of Olaf's other henchmen were already waiting at the long, black automobile, which was parked in front of the freaks' caravan. Hugo, Colette, and Kevin were crowded in the back seat with the two white-faced women, while Esmé Squalor sat in the front, with Sunny on her lap. The hook-handed man took the box out of the older Baudelaires' hands and threw it into the trunk while Count Olaf pointed to the caravan with his whip, which looked much shorter, and rough around the edges.

"You two will ride in that," he said. "We're

going to attach it to the automobile and pull you along with us."

"Isn't there room in the car?" Violet asked nervously.

"Don't be ridiculous," the hook-handed man said with a sneer. "It's too crowded. Good thing Colette is a contortionist, so she can curl into a ball at our feet."

"Chabo already gnawed my whip down so it could be used as a connecting rope," Count Olaf said. "I'll just tie the caravan to the car with a double slipknot, and then we'll ride off into the sunset."

"Excuse me," Violet said, "but I know a knot called the Devil's Tongue that I think will hold better."

"And if I remember the map correctly," Klaus said, "we should ride east until we find Stricken Stream, so we should drive *that* way, away from the sunset."

"Yes, yes, yes," Count Olaf said quickly. "That's what I meant. Tie it yourself if you want. I'll go start the engine."

Olaf tossed the rope to Klaus while the hook-handed man reached into the trunk again, and brought out a pair of walkie-talkies the children remembered from when they were living in Olaf's home. "Take one of these," he said, putting one in Violet's hand, "so we can contact you if we need to tell you something."

"Hurry up," Count Olaf snapped, taking the other walkie-talkie. "The air is filling with smoke."

The villain and his henchmen got into the automobile, and Violet and Klaus knelt down to attach the caravan. "I can't believe I'm using this knot to help Count Olaf," she said. "It feels like I'm using my inventing skills to participate in something wicked."

"We're all participating," Klaus said glumly. "Sunny used her teeth to turn that whip into a connecting rope, and I used my map skills to tell Olaf which direction to head."

"At least we'll get there, too," Violet said,

"and maybe one of our parents will be waiting for us. There. The knot's tied. Let's get in the caravan."

"I wish we were riding with Sunny," Klaus said.

"We are," Violet said. "We're not getting to the Mortmain Mountains the way we want, but we're getting there, and that's what counts."

"I hope so," Klaus said, and he and his sister stepped into the freaks' caravan and shut the door. Count Olaf started the engine of the car, and the caravan began to rock gently back and forth as the automobile pulled them away from the carnival. The hammocks swayed above the two siblings, and the rack of clothing creaked beside them, but the knot Violet had tied held fast, and the two vehicles began traveling in the direction Klaus had pointed.

"We might as well get comfortable," Violet said. "We'll be traveling a long time."

"All night at least," Klaus said, "and probably most of the next day. I hope they'll stop and share the food."

"Maybe we can make some hot chocolate later," Violet said.

"With cinnamon," Klaus said, smiling as he thought of Sunny's recipe. "But what should we do in the meantime?"

Violet sighed, and she and her brother sat down on a chair so she could lay her head on the table, which was shaking slightly as the caravan headed out into the hinterlands. The eldest Baudelaire put down the walkie-talkie next to the set of dominoes. "Let's just sit," she said, "and think."

Klaus nodded in agreement, and the two Baudelaires sat and thought for the rest of the afternoon, as the automobile pulled them farther and farther away from the burning carnival. Violet tried to imagine what the V.F.D. headquarters might look like, and hoped that one of their parents would be there. Klaus tried to imagine what Olaf and his troupe were talking about, and hoped that Sunny was not too frightened. And both the older Baudelaires thought about all that had happened at Caligari Carnival, and wondered whether or not they had done the right things. They had disguised themselves in order to find the answers to their questions, and now the answers were burning up under Madame Lulu's table, as her archival library went up in smoke. They had encouraged their coworkers to find employment someplace where they wouldn't be considered freaks, and now they had joined Count Olaf's evil troupe. And they had promised Madame Lulu that they would take her with them, so she could lead them to V.F.D. and become a noble person again, but she had fallen into the lion pit and become nothing but a meal. Violet and Klaus thought about all of the trouble they were in, and wondered if it was all due to simple misfortune, or if some of it was of their own devising. These were not the most pleasant thoughts in the world, but it still felt good to sit and think about them, instead of hiding and lying and frantically thinking up plans. It was peaceful to sit and think in the freaks' caravan, even when the caravan tilted slightly as they reached the beginning of the Mortmain Mountains and began to head uphill. It was so peaceful to sit and think that both Violet and Klaus felt as if they were waking up from a long sleep when Count Olaf's voice came out of the walkie-talkie.

"Are you there?" Olaf asked. "Press the red button and speak to me!"

Violet rubbed her eyes, picked up the walkie-talkie, and held it so both she and her brother could hear. "We're here," she said.

"Good," Count Olaf replied, "because I wanted to tell you that I learned something else from Madame Lulu."

"What did you learn?" Klaus asked.

There was a pause, and the two children could hear cruel peals of laughter coming from the small device in Violet's hand. "I learned that you are the Baudelaires!" Count Olaf cried in

triumph. "I learned that you three brats followed me here and tricked me with sneaky disguises. But I'm too clever for you!"

Olaf began to laugh again, but over his laughter the two siblings could hear another sound
that made them feel as shaky as the caravan. It
was Sunny, and she was whimpering in fear.

"Don't hurt her!" Violet cried. "Don't you
dare hurt her!"

"Hurt her?" Count Olaf snarled. "Why, I
wouldn't dream of hurting her! After all, I need
one orphan to steal the fortune. First I'm going
to make sure both of your parents are dead, and
then I'm going to use Sunny to become very,
very rich! No, I wouldn't worry about this buck-
toothed twerp—not yet. If I were you, I'd worry
about yourselves! Say bye-bye to your sister,
Baudebrats!"

"But we're tied together," Klaus said. "We
hitched our caravan to you."

"Look out the window," Count Olaf said,
and hung up the walkie-talkie. Violet and Klaus

looked at one another, and then staggered to their feet and moved the curtain away from the window. The curtain parted as if they were watching a play, and if I were you I would pretend that this is a play, instead of a book—perhaps a tragedy, written by William Shakespeare—and that you are leaving the theater early to go home and hide under a sofa, because you will recall that there was a certain expression that, I'm sorry to say, must be used three times before this story is over, and it is in the thirteenth chapter when this expression will be used for the third time. The chapter is very short, because the end of this story happened so quickly that it does not take many words to describe, but the chapter does contain the third occasion requiring the expression "the belly of the beast," and you would be wise to leave before the chapter begins, because that time didn't count.

Thirteen

With the curtain parted, Violet and Klaus
looked out the window and gasped at
what they saw. In front of them was
Count Olaf's long, black automobile,
winding its crooked way up the
road toward the peaks of
the Mortmain Mountains,
with the freaks' caravan
tied to the bumper.
They could not
see their baby
sister, who

was trapped in the front seat with Olaf and his villainous girlfriend, but they could imagine how frightened and desperate she was. But the older Baudelaires also saw something that made them frightened and desperate, and it was something they had never thought to imagine.

Hugo was leaning out of the back window of the automobile, his hump hidden in the over-sized coat Esmé Squalor had given him as a present, and he was holding tight to Colette's ankles. The contortionist had twisted her body around to the back of the car so that her head was lying on the middle of the trunk, between two of the bullet holes that had provided air for the Baudelaires on their way to Caligari Carnival. Like her coworker, Colette was also holding tight to someone's ankles—the ambi-dextrous ankles of Kevin, so that all three of Madame Lulu's former employees were in a sort of human chain. At the end of the chain were Kevin's hands, which were gripping a long, rusty knife. Kevin looked up at Violet and Klaus, gave them a triumphant grin, and brought the knife down as hard as he could on the knot Violet had tied.

The Devil's Tongue is a very strong knot, and normally it would take a while for a knife to saw through it, even if it was very sharp, but the equal strength in Kevin's two arms meant that the knife moved with a freakish power, instead of normally, and in an instant the knot was split in two.

"*No!*" Violet yelled.

"*Sunny!*" Klaus screamed.

With the caravan unhitched, the two vehicles began going in opposite directions. Count Olaf's car continued to wind its way up the mountain, but without anything pulling it, the caravan began to roll back down, the way a grapefruit will roll down a flight of stairs if you let it go, and there was no way for Violet or Klaus to steer or stop the caravan from the inside. The Baudelaires screamed again, all three of them, Violet and Klaus alone in the rattling caravan, and Sunny in the car full of villains, as the two vehicles slipped further and further away from each other, but even though Count Olaf was getting closer and closer to what he wanted and the older Baudelaires were getting further and further away, it seemed to the children that all three siblings were ending up at the same place. Even as Count Olaf's automobile slipped out of view, and the caravan began to slip on the bumpy road, it seemed to the Baudelaire orphans that they were all slipping into the belly of the beast, and that time, I'm sorry to say, counted very, very much.

LEMONY SNICKET

published his first book in 1999 and has not had a good night's sleep since. Once the recipient of several distinguished awards, he is now an escapee of several indistinguishable prisons. Early in his life, Mr. Snicket learned to reupholster furniture, a skill that turned out to be far more important than anyone imagined.

Visit him on the Web at www.lemonysnicket.com

BRETT HELQUIST

was born in Ganado, Arizona, and grew up in Orem, Utah. He studied hard to become an illustrator, but can't help wondering if he might have chosen to become something safer, like a pirate. Despite the risks, he continues to translate Lemony Snicket's odd findings into unusual pictures.

To My Kind E itor,

I hope you can read thi . The weather here is
so freezing that the ink in my typewriter ribbon
occasionally

                        . Here in the Valley of
Four   , the icy   has
      and the results are quite   .
  As my enemies draw closer, it is simply not safe
to place the entire manuscript of the Baudelaires'
                        , entitled THE
SLIPPERY SLOPE, in y
Instead, I am taking each of the thirteen chapte

in different places.
        "The world is
She will give you a key, which wi

                  the first chapter, as well as a
rare photogrsaph of a swarm of   , to help Mr.
Helquist with his illustrations. UNDER NO
CIRCUMSTANCES SHOULD YOU (

    trice.
    Remember, y   last hope that the tales
of the
to the general

i a   ue e ect,

I m ny   ick t